A Different Life

A Different Life

by Sheila Jacobs

CHRISTIAN FOCUS PUBLICATIONS

© 2000 Sheila Jacobs
ISBN 1-85792-590-4

Published by Christian Focus Publications Ltd,
Geanies House, Fearn, Tain, Ross-shire
IV20 1TW, Scotland, Great Britain
www.christianfocus.com
email: info@christianfocus.com

Cover illustration by Graham Kennedy, Allied Artists.
Cover design by Owen Daily.

Printed and bound by Cox & Wyman, Reading.

All rights reserved. No part of this publication may be reproduced, stored in a retrieval system, or transmitted, in any form or by any means, electronic, mechanical, photocopying, recording or otherwise, without prior permission of Christian Focus Publications.

My flesh and my heart may fail
but God is the strength of my heart
and my portion forever.

(Psalm 73:26)

THANKS

Huge thanks to all who have
prayed while I'm writing
and to my Mum, Mary Jacobs,
who consistently puts up with me.

CONTENTS

Oh, Amanda! 9
Changing 16
Smart Jeans and Bleached Hair 24
Aunty Ann Arrives 34
My Dear Relatives 44
The Black Dog 55
Cool 66
Problems 76
Life Stinks 87
By the River 97
Taking Sides 108
A Different Life 118

Oh, Amanda!

It was a Friday.

A bright, sunny Friday in September.

That was the day I changed. Or to be more accurate, began to change. Because, that day, things which hadn't seemed important before really began to matter.

Everything started out quite normally that morning. I woke up, and thanked God that we had a day off school whilst the teachers got to grips with some part of the curriculum they didn't understand, and thought they ought to know something about before they tried to teach it to us. I said 'morning' to Mum who was busy on the computer in the little spare room she called her office. Then I had some toast, and hung about a bit till it was time to meet my best friend.

"I'm going now, Mum!"

"What?" She looked up from the screen. "What - oh yes, you're going shopping with Amanda, aren't you?" Her forehead wrinkled. "Oh dear. I'm not sure it's quite safe, you two girls roaming around town on your own."

For a moment I thought she was going to insist she came with us - she had done until just recently, when she'd got a lot more work to do - but her fax machine burst into frenzied action and she looked harassed and said, "All right. But I don't want you hanging around the town all day! Come straight back.

9

And don't talk to any strangers on the bus!"

I forgot about Mum as I hurtled down the road to meet Amanda at the stop.

She wasn't there. I began to wonder if I'd got the wrong time.

Then, I spotted her, hurrying up the street.

"Hiya!" I said, "Here's the bus. You nearly missed it."

"I was on the phone," she told me, breathlessly.

We got on board, and Amanda was puffing and blowing so much she couldn't talk for a while. But even when she got her breath back, she didn't look quite herself. Her eyes seemed tremendously sparkly and her cheeks were more flushed than usual.

"Are you all right?" I asked, as the bus jolted along.

"Yep. Never better. Why?"

"You look a bit - I dunno - red."

She giggled.

"What's funny?"

"Nothing."

I knew that wasn't true. She was excited, I could tell. I figured out that it must be because she was going shopping, which she loved.

"I suppose we'll be spending most of our time in Fay's Fashions," I observed, unwrapping a piece of chewing gum, "But don't forget, I want to go to 'Sounds'. The new CD by 'The View'- "

"The View!" Amanda giggled again, "You don't still like them, do you, Sammy?" And I frowned. She was definitely acting oddly, because she had always liked The View as much as I did.

"Amanda, why are you being weird?"

"I'm not."

She was, though. She kept glancing at me as if she knew something I didn't know, and I got quite fed up with it. If she had some silly secret, I supposed she'd tell me, sometime, but I wasn't going to give her the satisfaction of thinking I was dying to know it. So I ignored her as the bus rolled on towards Millstead town centre, and she fidgeted, and sighed a few times, as I resolutely stared out of the window.

Amanda seemed to become more her usual self once we got off the bus. She chattered about the kind of dress she wanted to buy, and we trailed in and out of clothes shops, with Amanda scratching her head and pulling faces because she couldn't find anything she liked. Finally, we reached Fay's Fashions. Amanda eventually picked out a tiny shift dress, and I plonked myself down on a little plastic chair near the window to wait - and wait - and wait - whilst she went into a changing cubicle. And at that point in the day, life seemed boringly normal.

I idly watched people traipse by the store, listening to the clattering of feet on pavements. There were young women dragging reluctant infants and old women who all looked the same - permed hair and glasses - clutching shopping bags and talking to each other, probably about the price of eggs and other dreary stuff. I wondered why none of them had the ridiculous body shapes of the shop window dummies.

I unwrapped a piece of chewing gum.

"We don't allow the chewing of gum in Fay's Fashions!" said a beaky-nosed shop assistant, who was pretending to re-arrange clothes on the Sale Rail close by, but who was obviously just using that as an excuse to keep an eye on me and my gum. So I glared a bit and put the gum away. Then I checked my watch. I wondered what was wrong with Amanda's brain that it took her so long to try on a silly little dress. But at last, she appeared.

"Sammy! What d'you think?"

I blinked at her. She looked great. She twirled round a bit. The dress, with its tiny straps and shiny material, made her look tremendously slim and attractive. She'd undone her pony-tail, and her long fair hair was hanging loose round her shoulders.

In fact, she looked so good, I felt a twinge of jealousy. We'd shared fun and good times and a huge crush on the boys in The View. But on that Friday, I suddenly saw that something had happened to Amanda that I couldn't share at all. We were the same age - thirteen. But somehow she'd blossomed into this gorgeous girl and all I'd got were spots and greasy hair.

"How do I look?" asked Amanda, knowing perfectly well that she looked fantastic.

"All right," I said, grudgingly, "C'mon, will you just hurry up and buy the dress, so we can get to 'Sounds'?"

"Why don't you try something on, Sammy?"

"What? No. Got no money - as usual."

"Come on. Try something anyway. Just for a laugh."

"Oh, thanks!"

"No, I didn't mean it like that. But you know, you could look quite - er - nice - if you just got out of those tatty old jeans once in a while."

"Just get changed. I'm bored stiff."

She went back into the cubicle and pulled the curtain. I tried not to feel annoyed at what she'd said about me trying something on 'for a laugh'. The shop assistant was dealing with another customer, so I defiantly unwrapped some more gum and sulkily wondered whether I'd ever get to 'Sounds'.

Amanda came out of the cubicle again. She dimpled prettily at the assistant whose sour face broke into a beaming smile as she took Amanda's money.

"You've forgotten to tie your hair up," I pointed out, as we left the shop, "It's all over your face."

Amanda stopped and looked a bit awkward. "Don't be cross. But I don't think I've got time to go to 'Sounds'. Do you mind? I just want to go home."

"What!"

"I'm sorry."

"But I trailed around all those clothes shops with you! I don't see why -"

"Sammy, don't start an argument. I just want to go home."

"Amanda! You're so selfish!"

"Selfish! I've had to put up with your Mum coming shopping with us week after week until just lately!"

"Oh - I thought you liked my Mum!"

Amanda sighed. "I do. It's just - oh, look. If you must know, I'm going out tonight, that's why I wanted the dress, and that's why I want to go home early, to get ready."

"But it's only half-past one!"

"Yes, well. I want to wash my hair, have a bath..."

"Why? Why all the fuss? Amanda, where are

you going tonight?"

"I'm going to a party." Her eyes twinkled.

"A party!"

"Mmm. And guess what?" she blurted out, "Tank Willis is going, too!"

"Tank Willis?" I thought of him. He was in the year above us at school. He was thick-set (that's why they called him 'Tank'), short, and had a big chin. "So what, Amanda?"

"Well, he phoned me, just now, and sort of asked me to go with him!"

"Did he?" I laughed. "What did you say? 'Get lost, you creep'?"

She looked annoyed. "No, I didn't. I said I'd go with him."

I goggled in disbelief. So that was why she was so excited! Anyone would think that Tank Willis was a heart-throb! Just why Amanda seemed so pleased about going to a party with him, I couldn't imagine!

"Amanda, you don't like Tank! You've never said anything to me about liking him! I thought you liked Lennie from The View! You said no boy could ever match up to Lennie!"

"Lennie from The View! Oh Sammy!" She tossed her hair.

"But why didn't you tell me?"

"I didn't think you'd understand."

"I don't. Tank Willis! He's awful. Tell me you're joking!"

"Sammy! Tank's not awful. I knew it'd be a mistake telling you he'd asked me. I thought you might be jealous."

"Jealous!" My jaw dropped. Jealous of Amanda

going out with a twit like Tank who thought it was clever to chuck stones at the ducks on Millstead Park pond? She was mad - and I was about to tell her so - but she was swiftly walking off in the direction of the bus station, and I had to hurry to catch up with her. We caught our bus and sat down. I didn't know what to say; if I said anything detrimental about Tank, she might think I really was jealous. So I gaped a bit like a fish and then unwrapped some more gum and chewed furiously.

"Don't worry, Sammy." She patted my shoulder, and I'm sure she didn't mean to sound so smug. "I bet you'll meet someone nice too - one day!"

"Nice!" I thought of Tank and the ducks and almost swallowed my gum.

"Tank said would I like to go and watch him play five-a-side football tomorrow. That means I won't be able to come to your house for tea, Sammy." She shook her loose hair back. "You don't mind - do you? I'm sorry."

"Oh, Amanda!"

I really looked forward to Amanda coming to tea on Saturdays. She batted her eyelashes at me and I sat back in my seat, totally unable to work out why my best friend would rather spend time with that terrible Tank than with me. And I must've seemed pretty mortified, because in between looking smug and excited, Amanda almost looked genuinely sorry.

Changing

"How's Amanda?"

"Weird."

"What?"

"She won't be coming to tea tomorrow."

"Oh! Why not? You two haven't fallen out, I hope?"

I shovelled ham and chips into my mouth.

"She's got a boyfriend."

"A boyfriend!" Mum shook her head. "Well, I'm thankful you're not remotely interested in boys."

I didn't like to tell her that most of the girls in my class had boyfriends. In fact, I hadn't really thought much about it before today.

Half an hour later, we trudged off up the street to the old people's flats in Walters Road. Friday was Mum's Bible Study and Prayer Meeting night, and it was usually held in old Mr Upson's flat. I hated going, but Mum insisted I did because, for reasons she never explained, she didn't like me being in the house alone in the evenings. I usually had to take my homework, and I always had a problem doing it because Mr Upson's flat was very small and the heating was always on, even in late summer, so it was hot and uncomfortable - and always smelled of boiled chicken. And because Mr Upson was a bit deaf, the people in the meeting tended to shout a lot. Their voices thudded through the thin walls into the kitchen, where I was normally parked at the greasy blue formica-covered table wrestling with various dreary subjects.

We arrived, and I shuffled into Mr Upson's kitchen. There was the boiled chicken smell again. I felt sick. Mum asked if I was all right, and I thought about mentioning the smell, but Mr Upson poked his kind old face around the door and smiled so sweetly I didn't have the heart. They disappeared into the living room with several other people including the minister.

I sighed, and rummaged in my bag for the English homework I had been trying to put off doing. We had to write a ridiculous composition about the opening chapters of the most boring Victorian novel I'd ever read in my life. I stared at the same paragraph for ten minutes as the boom of loud voices began. It was no use, I couldn't concentrate. Besides, I had other things on my mind. I put the book down.

Boyfriends! Just about everyone had a boyfriend. Well, apart from Lizzy who was a swot, and Kerry who was so obsessed with horses no boy stood a chance, and Cody who was just plain unattractive. Oh, and me. Was I unattractive, too? I stood up, and stared at myself in Mr Upson's old mirror which was hanging above the table. Big, owlish, slightly short-sighted eyes - straight, lank, light brown hair. I seemed to be getting more freckles than ever. And my ears stuck out.

"That mirror's ancient," I told myself, "It's distorted."

I tossed my hair like I'd seen Amanda do earlier. My hair covered my ears, now, but unfortunately it covered my eyes too. I pushed it back and looked closely at myself. I wasn't getting more freckles, after all. Just a new crop of spots. I wondered if we had any anti-spot-zapping cream at home. I unwrapped some chewing-gum, and sat down again and tried to read.

Then it happened.

I really wasn't eavesdropping. But with the thin walls, and loud voices, I could hardly have missed what my mum was saying.

"Yes, a boyfriend. And she's only thirteen."

"Oh, that's nothing, nowadays! My little granddaughter is just eleven, and she's got a boyfriend!" said Mr Upson's voice, "All she talks about is fashion and make-up!"

"I can't approve of make-up on children. It makes them look tarty. Oh! Sorry, minister - I don't mean to be offensive. But I was seventeen before I had my first boyfriend, and that was Samantha's father! What? No, no. No trouble at all. Samantha's not interested in boys. She's a good girl. Loves church and the youth club and school. She's just started going off on little shopping trips with her friend - quite an adventure for her. Yes, I have no problems at all. Quite a saintly child! But then, she's young for her age, thank God. I wouldn't be surprised if she still plays with her dolls when I'm not looking."

I was so horrified my book fell with a loud bang onto the floor.

"Mum! How could you!"

Young for her age! Still plays with dolls! I was mortified. What an insult! Was that what Mum really thought of me? Fancy telling all those people such a thing!

"Samantha? What was that noise?"

My mother had appeared in the doorway. I

looked at her and felt an unusual surge of anger.

"Mum, I need a book I've left at home." A lie! I'd never lied to Mum before. But if I didn't get out of the flat right then, that minute, I felt I'd explode with rage, indignation and sheer embarrassment.

"Left it at home? Well, that's a bit silly, isn't it? I suppose you'll have to run and get it." Mum handed me her key. "Do you want me to come with you?"

"No!" I said, exasperated, "Of course I don't!"

"All right! There's no need to shout! Be quick then, straight there, and be careful - "

I was out of that flat before she could say another word. I clutched the key in my sweaty palm and rushed down the street. Mum's words, "Do you want me to come with you?" echoed in my mind. I had a horrific thought. I supposed Amanda would be walking home from school with Tank in future. If Mum found out I was walking home from school alone, surely she wouldn't start to do what she used to do before I met Amanda - wait for me by the school gates!

"She'd better not!"

I gritted my teeth. Why had she trailed round town with me and Amanda for so long? She was too over-protective. Really, it was a bit embarrassing, now I thought about it. It was as if she thought I was a child. Well, she did, didn't she? Dolls! Young for her age! What a cheek! I wasn't young for my age. Was I? Well, if I was, I wouldn't be any more! Maybe it was time I matured. I thought of how gorgeous Amanda had looked that afternoon. Tank Willis was totally ghastly, but at least Amanda had a boyfriend! Maybe I ought to think about getting one, as well! Yes, I decided - it was time to re-vamp my image. I'd start with the spots.

I got home, went into the bathroom, and rummaged about in the cupboard. I was sure I'd seen some tubes of cream lying around ages ago. Surely one of those would zap spots. I did find a few tubes, but they were ointments to put on insect bites. Then I found an old make-up bag of Mum's. I opened it. Out dropped an ancient black eyeliner pencil and the remains of a bright red lipstick.

Young for her age!

"I bet I look really grown-up with a bit of lipstick on!"

I couldn't remember Mum wearing eyeliner or scarlet lipstick or any kind of make-up at all so they must have been antiques. Never mind. I outlined my lips in red. My face disappeared immediately and all I could see was a big red mouth and teeth covered in lipstick. I tried circling my eyes with the eyeliner. But instead of looking darkly smouldering like the girls in the kind of magazines Amanda brought to school - or even looking 'tarty' - I looked like a cross between a panda and a nightmare, with huge, unnaturally red lips.

I wiped my hand across my mouth. My fingers came away scarlet. Frantically, I scrubbed at the lipstick. I couldn't believe how much was coming off. I didn't think I'd put that much on. It was the same with the eyeliner.

I couldn't go back to Mr Upson's flat looking like this. Mum would be aghast and might even get her friends to start praying for me.

"Amanda's so lucky!" I grumbled - and then I

remembered that Mum said we shouldn't say 'lucky' because there was no such thing as luck. "Well, she is, though!" I said, defiantly. After all, Amanda's mum actually encouraged her to wear mascara. She treated her like an adult. She even had her own TV in her bedroom.

We weren't as well off as Amanda's family because there was just the two of us; Mum supported us by doing freelance accounting and book-keeping, and she worked really hard, but we always seemed to get the necessities of life without too many of the luxuries. I was keen to get a paper round, but Mum wouldn't hear of it, and never explained why. Perhaps she thought I was too young to handle other people's newspapers, I thought, grimly. Amanda didn't have a paper round, but then, she had relatives who were always handing her wads of money as well as quite a generous allowance from her parents. I got a pittance, which, if you look it up in a dictionary, means 'inadequate wages'.

Still, I'd always said to myself that I didn't particularly want luxuries like a TV in my room. I wouldn't really have time to watch much of it; we got so much homework, and anyway, I had to be in bed by nine-thirty.

Amanda didn't have to be in bed by nine-thirty.

"Plays with dolls!"

It hadn't seemed to matter before that Mum was a bit strict and old-fashioned and out-of-step. She was different from my other friends' parents, but I had always thought different was better. After all, Mum said we were Christians. She also said she knew what was best, and I trusted her. Did that make me 'saintly'?

21

I didn't want to be saintly. It sounded horrible, like some little prig with a halo.

There were quite a few things I wasn't happy with, now I thought about it. For a start, Mum didn't much like me playing The View CDs; she said they weren't very spiritual and I shouldn't idolise them, which is why I couldn't put some really good The View posters Amanda had given me, up on my bedroom wall. Also, Mum didn't really like me going to the cinema with Amanda and there were certain films she simply would not let me see. Sometimes, when I was flopping in front of the TV on a Saturday evening, Mum switched the channel abruptly and said I shouldn't watch whatever it was I'd had on. I wasn't allowed to watch it at all on a Sunday. Or go to the shops. Or do anything apart from go to church. Twice.

I didn't mind church. I liked it. The people were nice, and I'd always loved hearing the stories about Jesus - especially when I was small. And I did like the youth club. Most of the kids were younger than me - well, all of them were - but it was fun, although it wasn't particularly amusing last Christmas when I'd suffered the indignity of having to be Joseph in the nativity play because none of the boys would agree to be 'married' to the objectionable girl who was playing Mary. Everybody had called me The Beard for ages afterwards.

I had a worrying thought. Maybe going to the youth club every Thursday had made me young for my age.

I washed my face. I didn't look so bad, now; there were still slight traces of black round my eyes, and my lips were a bit redder than usual. I thought I looked older in a subtle kind of way and felt a rush of excitement.

There was the sound of frantic knocking on the front door.

"Oh no! I'll bet that's Mum!"

I shoved the make-up into the bag and pushed it back into the cupboard.

"Oh help! Will she notice? I'll have to bluff it out."

I very slowly went down the stairs and calmly opened the door. Maybe Mum wouldn't notice the make-up but would just think I looked more mature all of a sudden.

"Samantha!" She stared at me. "Darling, I thought something was wrong. Why didn't you tell me you weren't feeling well? Love, you look so heavy-eyed, and your poor swollen lips! You must be allergic to something you've eaten. Don't worry, if you don't feel any better by the morning, we'll go to the doctor!"

Yes, that Friday was the day I decided to change.

The only problem was, how was I going to manage to grow up without Mum noticing and putting a stop to it?

Smart Jeans and Bleached Hair

Looks.

That was the important thing, I decided. My looks.

I was staring at some really horrendous charcoal drawings of something that looked like a witch. It was me. The Art teacher, Miss Morris, put a comforting hand on my shoulder.

I grimaced. Yes - my looks. I'd been wondering all week where to start in my campaign to Grow Up. Now I knew for sure.

Miss Morris had picked me out as the Subject in Life Drawing that Thursday, because she said I had a far away expression that would be interesting to capture. It was far away all right - it had been for several days now, since I'd been wondering how I could change. I didn't mind being the Subject. It gave me a good excuse to sit still, uninterrupted, and think. So the others tried to draw me in charcoal, tongues stuck out in concentration, and I thought about my face, my hair, my life. I didn't even hear Debi Daley ask 'Do we have to draw her spots?' although Amanda assured me she did say that - which was typical of Debi, who was the sort of girl who was very pretty but not very tactful.

"Don't worry, Sammy," said Debi, as she showed me the ghoulish effigy she'd drawn, "You don't really look as bad as that. Not really and truly. Honestly. You don't, Sammy." And you could just tell she thought I jolly well did.

I was still thinking about that picture as I was coming out of the sweet shop on my way home from school, and I suppose I must've been really distracted, because I bumped into someone. Or rather, someone bumped into me.

My vision was filled with a white shirt for a moment, he mumbled "Sorry" and the next minute I was outside, on the pavement, glancing over my shoulder. I only saw the back of him - a young guy with bleached hair. Bleached hair! What an idea! I tossed my ice-cream wrapper into the bin and stood there for a bit, wondering how I could dye my hair blonde gradually so Mum would think it was naturally turning fair.

"Oops!"

Someone bashed my arm. Some of my ice-cream finished up on my nose.

"Oi!" I said.

"Sorry again!"

It was that guy with the bleached hair. He'd come out of the shop and chucked something into the bin. I caught a flash of very white, very straight teeth.

"I keep getting in your way, don't I!" he said.

I was going to say, "Yes you do, you're dead clumsy!", but strangely I couldn't quite find the words, and finished up muttering, "It's OK," and feeling myself go red. He smiled again.

He was quite a bit older than me - about eighteen, I thought - but never in my life had I felt so stunned by a smile as I did right then. The boy was totally gorgeous. Much more gorgeous than anyone

I'd ever seen before in my life; yes, he was even better looking than Lennie from The View. And he was miles better than any of the spotty boys in my year at school - I'd never fancied any of them, they were pests, only good for a kick-about on the recreation ground.

I watched him walk on ahead of me. I remembered that dazzling smile, and my heart skipped a beat. He'd smiled at me! Wow! I felt a bit breathless and couldn't finish my ice-cream.

I followed him around the corner. He was heading towards our estate. To my surprise, he turned into Wingold Way - my own street.

"Well!" I said to myself, "Look at that!"

He'd disappeared into number 4. Next door to our house.

Of course, I thought. He must be one of our new neighbours.

Up until then, I hadn't taken a lot of notice of the newcomers. They'd moved in the previous Saturday. We'd watched the removal van pull up, and Mum had wondered out loud if they came from anywhere nice and had actually baked some fairy cakes to welcome them. But she'd changed her mind abruptly when Mrs Kettle from over the road came round and told us that there were three men sharing the house and they'd only moved from Radley Street - a mile away.

Then the vehicles had turned up, one by one: in the drive was a red Vauxhall with a crumpled right wing; on the road, a works' van with 'H and H - High Quality Window Sealant' scrawled on the side. There was an old two-tone VW camper van on the front lawn. Oh, and a motorbike. Mrs Kettle came round again and said she hoped the street wasn't turning into a scrap yard.

There was a note on our front door. It was from Mum. There had been a crisis at one of her clients' firms in town. Usually, she juggled her hours so that she was always home when I got in from school. The hurriedly scribbled note suggested that today I should go to Mrs Kettle's until she came back. But I knew the flower-pot where Mum kept her spare key so I launched a bid for adulthood and independence and let myself into the house.

I shot upstairs, and went into her bedroom, the room with the best view of the street. I pressed my nose to the window and eyed number 4. As I watched, the motorbike drew up, ridden by a man with an orange crash helmet. He got off the bike, and momentarily turned his face towards me. I shrank behind the curtain. I didn't want anyone thinking I was nosy.

He was quite old. I wondered if he was Bleached Hair's dad.

Bleached Hair! What a heart-throb! What was his real name? Probably something romantic like Tristram or Miles or Julian. He'd never want to be known as 'Tank'. I had a wild thought. If only Bleached Hair was my boyfriend! I could just imagine Amanda's eyes going completely round and goggly when she saw me with such a handsome boy! And Debi Daley - what would she think? What fun to cruise past her with an adoring Bleached Hair on my arm! My heart started thumping with excitement. How amazing that Bleached Hair had turned up right now when I'd decided to grow up properly! I felt slightly awestruck. Maybe it was meant to be! But my heart sank slightly when I realised that even if he did like me, Mum would probably go into a dead faint at the thought of me going out on a date with him.

I sauntered downstairs. I had some homework to do before dinner. It was youth club night tonight. But as I opened my books, I found I just couldn't concentrate. All I could see was that bleached hair and wonderful smile. Twenty minutes later, Mum came in, filling the house with a mouth-watering aroma as she slapped fish and chips from the shop down onto plates.

"What a day!" she said.

She looked tired. She didn't ask whether I'd been round to Mrs Kettle's. She stifled a yawn as she sat down.

"Did you have a nice day at school?"

"OK." I sprinkled vinegar over my chips. "Mum, I saw one of the new neighbours today."

"Mmm?"

"He's about eighteen. I bet he goes to the sixth form college."

This was a complete guess. I just wanted to find out if Mum knew anything about the new neighbours, without arousing her suspicions regarding my interest in Bleached Hair. But Mum didn't say anything. She just tucked into her fish.

"It's funny," I said, as casually as I could, "But they've moved in right next door, and we don't even know their names, do we?"

"No." Mum looked guilty. "I've been so busy. And I didn't want to seem - hmm. Perhaps we should go round and introduce ourselves."

"Oh yes. Yes, mmm. I think we should."

"Pass the vinegar, Sam."

"When?"

"What? Now - please - before my fish goes cold."

"No, I mean when are we going to introduce ourselves?"

"Eh?"

"After tea?"

"Samantha, that's a nice thought, but I'm very tired. Maybe tomorrow."

"Tomorrow, then."

I buttered another piece of bread and butter and tried to look cool.

"Does Mrs Kettle know anything about them?"

"What?"

"Mrs Kettle. She knows everything about everybody. She says curiosity's in her genes because her father was a spy for MI5."

"You don't want to believe everything you hear. Remember Mrs Kettle's interested in amateur dramatics. Have you finished your homework? It's youth club. Make sure you get a lift home with Bob."

Mum always insisted I got a lift home with Bob, the youth leader, even though the club was held in the church hall which was only next door to the sweet shop, five minutes' walk away. 'Plays with dolls!' popped into my brain, and I left the table. The feeling of annoyance was still there later on as I said goodbye.

"Are you wearing your best jeans, Samantha?" Mum asked.

"Er - yes."

"Isn't that a bit silly? You play all those rowdy

29

games. I think you'd better wear your old tracksuit bottoms like you usually do."

I hovered in the doorway. I wanted to wear my best jeans just in case Bleached Hair was looking out of his window as I went past.

"I can't," I said, half-heartedly.

"Why ever not?"

"I just can't."

"What do you mean, can't?"

"Oh, Mum! I'm just late, that's all."

She checked her watch. "No you're not. Quick, change, love. You've got ten minutes."

I thought about arguing, but Mum looked weary and I didn't want to upset her. She worked so hard to keep us. And I didn't want to have to explain about wanting to wear something nice just in case the boy next door saw me. After all, I was 'saintly' and not interested in boys...wasn't I?

So, I changed, felt cross about it and slammed the front door as I left the house.

I just hoped Bleached Hair wouldn't see me in these old tracksuit bottoms.

I was so fed up with having to change my jeans that by the time I got to the youth club, I was in a really bad mood. I stalked into the hall.

"Ah, here she is!" cried Bob, and about a dozen little kids cheered.

Normally, I would have smiled. But today I just felt irritated.

"Samantha Jones!" Bob glanced down at his register and put a tick next to my name. It was just like being at school. Suddenly, I felt cross about that, too.

Bob was bouncing around now, organising a game. He was old, twenty-five, but he was fun, and he told the most interesting stories. His brother was a missionary, and Bob himself had worked with a famous travelling evangelist. He'd preached the gospel and actually seen sick people get healed. He acted as if he and Jesus were great friends - as if he really knew him, and he wasn't just someone who featured in Bible stories.

However, today I wasn't thinking about Bouncing Bob or Jesus or silly games; I was thinking about smart jeans, although I found myself forgetting about them when the first game began. I usually enjoyed the games Bob made us play. We played them before the serious bit - a story from the Bible, and some teaching to do with God and Jesus. But as I started to have a good time, hopping around on one leg singing a song, I recalled Mum's words again - 'young for her age'. What would Bleached Hair think if he could see me now? I was too old for stupid games. They were childish. I stopped playing and sat on the stage.

"Sammy!" said Bob, red-faced and out of breath. And all of a sudden I thought he was childish, too. "Sammy! What's up?"

"Nothing."

"Are you OK?"

I was going to say, "I don't want to hop around singing with a bunch of ten and eleven-year-olds anymore. All right?" But I didn't have the heart. Bob might be childish, but he was very nice - he always reminded me of a great big bouncy golden retriever, with friendly brown eyes and lots of energy. "I don't feel - " I stopped. If I said "I don't feel well" he'd pray for me. I didn't want to be prayed for.

"I just feel tired today," I lied, and felt guilty.

"OK, Sammy. You sit there for a bit."

They carried on playing. One of the kids, a wan-faced child I'd rather horribly, and secretly, labelled Drippy Dinah, came over, and took my hand, concerned.

"Shall I sit with you, Sammy?"

I shook my head, impatiently. Then I felt a bit bad. The kid was being so kind and I was being so stand-offish. But I couldn't seem to help myself.

At last, Bob and the others collapsed on the floor and he got out his big Bible and read something from Luke's gospel. It was the part where Jesus taught about prayer, and finished up with 'Ask and it will be given to you; seek and you will find; knock and the door will be opened to you. For everyone who asks receives; he who seeks finds; and to him who knocks, the door will be opened.'

I switched off a bit while he was reading because I'd heard that passage stacks of times before. Bob put his Bible down and started giving a little chat about the importance of praying and not giving up, and how crucial it was to pray for each other's needs, and I half-listened, wishing he'd wrap it up because I wanted to get home. Truthfully, I wasn't that interested in what he was saying because I rather arrogantly assumed I'd heard it all before, and that Bob had nothing new to say about prayers so far as I was concerned: I did pray, after all - sometimes - usually in the form of a Shopping List, which didn't seem to work - and I did say 'thank you God' if something good happened. If I remembered.

I was just wondering if I'd see Bleached Hair tomorrow, and racking my brain to think of a way to find out his name, when something Bob said cut through my thoughts.

"And we really mustn't forget to pray for people we know who don't know Jesus. I mean, people who haven't yet asked Jesus into their hearts. People who don't know him as their own, personal Saviour and Friend."

I glanced up, sharply. Bob wasn't looking at me. Nobody was. They all had their eyes shut, now, and Drippy Dinah was thanking Jesus for being her Friend. I suddenly remembered Mum telling me when I was six that Jesus was my Friend, too. A thought drifted into my mind that Jesus had seemed more real to me when I was a little kid than he did now I was older. I didn't know why. I wasn't sure it mattered. After all, I was still a Christian, wasn't I? I went to church and everything.

And so I dismissed whatever it was that had momentarily disturbed me, and my mind turned again to what I considered were really important things - like smart jeans and Bleached Hair.

Aunty Ann Arrives

Mrs Kettle was a widow. She was ancient, about forty. She wasn't a Christian, but Mum had often said she was a Respectable Lady even if she did tend to Flirt. I was twelve before I found out what Flirt meant and I was quite relieved when I did, because I thought it meant something totally different to do with her digestion.

When I got home from school that Friday, she was in our kitchen, her gold-rimmed glasses glinting, and her over-made-up eyes flashing.

"Hello," I said, coming in and dumping my schoolbag by the fridge.

Mum was sitting opposite Mrs Kettle, leaning on the table, drinking a cup of tea.

"I've met the new neighbour, Sam," said Mum.

I sat down, feeling disappointed. I'd really hoped that Mum and I might go round to number 4 this evening and introduce ourselves. I might have even got another smile from Bleached Hair - still, at least I could find out something about him.

"Mrs Kettle introduced me just now."

"He's very pleasant," said Mrs Kettle, "about forty-five, wouldn't you say, Katy?"

"Something like that, I suppose."

Oh! They must mean Bleached Hair's dad!

"His name's Mr Price," said Mum.

Price! I knew his surname!

"Jack," Mrs Kettle's eyes twinkled. "He said to

34

call him 'Jack', dear."

"Yes, I know he did."

And something told me she'd be calling him 'Mr Price'.

"He isn't related to the others, apparently," said Mrs Kettle, "They're lodgers. The one with the van's called Des."

I sighed. I hadn't found out anything about Bleached Hair at all - except he was a lodger.

"Mr Price is a Manager. He had the afternoon off. I believe he's divorced," said Mrs Kettle, "But I shall certainly find out more as time goes by."

"Well," said Mum, clearing the cups away, "Ann'll be here shortly. We'd better start getting prepared."

"Oh!" With all the excitement about Bleached Hair, I had completely forgotten about my Aunty Ann's impending visit. She was travelling up from Kent for the weekend. I groaned.

"Sorry, dear?" said Mrs Kettle.

"Nothing," I said. And I nearly groaned again as I remembered the last time Aunty Ann came. She'd spent the entire time moaning about breaking up with her latest boyfriend, Bo (which she pronounced 'Beau' and not B.O.), who'd apparently talked a lot about his Cosmic Energy but couldn't find enough of it to get a job.

"And there's great news, Sam," Mum said, brightly, "Ann's bringing your cousins with her!"

"Oh no!" I said, and added, hastily, "I mean, oh, good!"

"They'll be staying with me, dear!" said Mrs Kettle, winking at me, "So you won't have to share

35

your bedroom or anything!"

I was tempted to say, 'thank goodness for small mercies'. I supposed Aunty Ann would be sleeping on the futon in Mum's little office. At least bossy Kendra and dopey Dorian wouldn't be taking over our house, too.

"It's very kind of you," Mum was saying to Mrs Kettle, "Ann really does leave these things till the last minute. Her ex-husband was going to have the children, but he's had to rush off on some sort of business commitment in Belgium. So, when she phoned - "

"No problem, dear!" Mrs Kettle patted Mum's arm. "I shall enjoy the company!"

I stifled another groan. I would have preferred to have spent my weekend thinking about ways to improve my appearance and trying to get a glimpse of Bleached Hair, rather than entertain irritating relatives I didn't much like.

"You'll have someone to play with, Sam!" Mum smiled at me.

"Play with!" I said.

"Oh - of course, they're a bit old for playing," said Mum.

"So am I!" I protested, but Mum was talking again.

"I can't say I totally approve of how my sister's bringing up her children," she said to Mrs Kettle, "It's her business, of course. But do you know, her daughter was wearing so much make-up the last time she visited, I longed to wash it all off! Such a fresh young face, plastered with all that - " Mum stopped. Mrs Kettle, of course, was plastered with 'all that'. But Mrs Kettle didn't seem to take it personally.

"So how old are they, exactly, Katy?" she asked.

"The girl's nearly sixteen, and the boy's a year older."

They turned up at half past six in Aunty Ann's rusty old estate car.

"Ann!" said my mother, as the car door creaked open.

"Darling!" said Ann.

I watched from the front door as my cousin Kendra stepped out of the car. She wasn't exactly beautiful, but she always seemed to look glamorous and sophisticated. Dorian emerged from the back seat, tall, lanky, scruffy and half-asleep.

A large blob shot across the road. Mrs Kettle was coming to welcome the visitors.

"Darling!" Aunty Ann had spotted me. She rushed up and planted a dry kiss on my cheek. She'd had beads put into her long straggly hair and they banged against my nose.

Kendra sauntered up with a glacial half smile.

"All right, Sam?"

She ambled into the hall, leaving her brother to lug the cases in. He looked at me out of dopey, heavy-lidded eyes and raised an eyebrow which was his way of saying hello.

"You look wonderful!" Aunty Ann was saying to Mum.

"Thanks. Cup of tea?"

"Ah, I only drink herbal nowadays. I've got a packet somewhere. Here we are. Improves your circulation, revives your energy."

"Oh?"

37

"Darling, I've got such exciting news for you," said Aunty Ann, her intense dark eyes fixing Mum with a dramatic stare, "I've found myself!"

I blinked and Mrs Kettle looked astounded.

"Gracious!" she said, "Were you lost?"

Ann ignored her. She gripped my mum's arm. "Negative energies bombarding our souls! We've got to get rid of them! I'll tell you all about it."

"Dorian!" said Mrs Kettle, with a wide smile, "Come across the road. I expect you'd like to unpack."

Dorian shrugged his shoulders, lazily, and allowed Mrs Kettle to propel him across the street, chattering incessantly about what a nice strong young man he was and how she had some shelves which needed fixing. We didn't see him again that evening. Sadly, Kendra chose not to follow him. Instead, she asked to borrow the loo, which I thought was odd, because it's not exactly something you can 'borrow'.

"Ann," said Mum, "I expect you're hungry after your journey."

"Darling," said Aunty Ann, flopping down on the sofa, "Those motorway service stations are full of bad vibes. But wonderful clean lavatories and quite reasonable vegetarian burgers."

"So you don't want a sandwich," said Mum.

"No, thanks."

"No trouble, Ann. I'm making some for Sam and myself."

"No, darling, really. Let me tell you all about finding myself."

I decided to leave them to it. I crept upstairs and found Kendra peering into my room.

"I can't believe you still like The View, Sam."

"How d'you know?"

"I found that rolled-up poster at the back of your wardrobe."

"What!"

Kendra looked at me.

"I'd far rather stay over here with you lot," she said, "I don't really want to stay with that old trout over the road."

"Well, that's sad, but there's no room."

"You could sleep on the couch downstairs."

"What a cheek!"

She looked down at me. She really was tall and very slim.

"When did I last see you? June? Hmm. You've put on weight."

"No I haven't!"

"Do you still chew all that gum?"

"So what if I do?"

Kendra smiled in her snooty way, and wandered over to the window.

"Coo!" she said, "Who is THAT?"

I went up behind her, and drew a sharp breath. Bleached Hair was in his garden, hanging out a pair of jeans on the washing-line!

"Wow," said Kendra, "He's not bad, is he!"

I felt a twinge of jealousy. Kendra had had loads of boyfriends. She'd told me before that Aunty Ann had said it was important for her to know a lot of boys before she met Someone to Settle Down With. I certainly didn't want her getting to know Bleached Hair! He was mine! Still - she was only here for a couple of days, and she lived in Kent. She had no chance at all with Bleached Hair.

39

"He's just a neighbour," I said, "Let's go downstairs."

"All right, don't shove me." She stared at me. "You'd look quite nice, you know, Sam, even pretty, if you lost a bit of weight. Oh, and if you did something about your skin."

And I'm ashamed to admit that I hoped she'd trip and fall downstairs.

Mum had made some tomato sandwiches, which I was about to devour with gusto because I was starving. But I was aware of Kendra watching me so I only ate a couple and refused Mum's delicious home-made carrot cake. Mum asked if I was feeling OK and Aunty Ann said she thought I looked a bit pasty-faced and tired, and I wished with all my heart that I didn't have an aunt and cousins. Then Aunty Ann said that if she and Kendra had been hungry, they still wouldn't have touched the sandwiches because they weren't the 'right sort of bread' nor the cake, because the carrots weren't organic.

"Well, I knew you'd become vegetarian," said Mum, stiffly, obviously a bit upset at the criticism of her food, "But I thought - "

Aunty Ann interrupted her and said she and Kendra were on the WOOF diet - Wheat-free Organic Only Fibre diet. Kendra smiled sweetly at me and pointedly said it was a brilliant diet because it made you lose weight and stopped you getting spots. I said I thought the WOOF diet sounded like something Mrs Kettle's little dog Flossie might eat, which made Mum glare at me, and my aunt and cousin looked at me as if I were a silly kid. Then Aunty Ann recovered, and began talking in her machine-gun-fire sort of way about finding herself, and Mum and I soon realised she'd become deeply involved in all sorts of weird New Age stuff and alternative therapies.

"It was Bo's influence, of course," she gushed, "He expanded my mind and introduced me to all sorts of things. When he left me - to go off hugging trees with that frightful Noleen Riley from the bakery - I decided that he might've gone, but he'd left a unique spiritual influence, and I decided to explore it. I'm on a journey, you see. We all are."

"Mum's really into spiritual things now," Kendra said, rather unnecessarily.

"Yes, I'm a spiritual being," said Ann, "It fascinates me."

"Well, Ann, you know, I'm a bit surprised," said Mum, "When I've tried to talk to you about spiritual things before, you've never really been interested."

Aunty Ann seemed genuinely puzzled for a moment, and then she laughed. "Oh! Darling! You're talking about going to church, aren't you!" And after that, it became clear that the one spiritual thing she wasn't fascinated by was Christianity and Jesus which she patronisingly dismissed as Narrow.

"You know the trouble with Christians!" she said, airily, "They don't believe there's any other way to reach God but their way! Narrow, narrow, narrow!"

"Yes, but Ann," said Mum, trying to sound calm and patient but obviously getting a bit irritated, "Jesus himself said 'I am the way, and the truth, and the life. No-one comes to the Father except through me.' What he was saying was, he's the only way. The only door."

Aunty Ann waved her hand dismissively.

"Ann," said Mum, warming to her theme, "We

can't reach God on our own. All the good works we ever do will never make us right with a perfect God or cancel out the things we've done wrong. The only way to be right with God and have a friendship with him is to come to Jesus - Jesus took the punishment for all the things we've said and done wrong, when he died on the cross. Then he came back to life. He's alive and real today and we can know him. Jesus invites us to come to him to be right with God...when we do, he forgives our wrongs, and gives us a new, clean sort of life, his Holy Spirit living in us, helping us live to please him, and making his Presence very real to us."

"Katy," said Ann, screwing up her nose, "You don't seem to think there are any other avenues of spirituality to explore! Everything revolves around your Jesus!"

"That's true," said Mum, nodding, "It all depends on what you think of Jesus. When you look at what he said, you have to ask yourself whether he was mad, or bad, or whether he meant what he said - was he truly who he claimed to be? The Son of God? I think so."

"Well, I don't," said Ann, shortly, "And I still think you're narrow, narrow, narrow. After all, we're all still searching for Truth, darling."

"Christians aren't. They've found the Truth. Jesus."

I stared at Mum in admiration. For all her faults and foibles, she really did have great faith.

I suddenly found myself wishing I could speak with such conviction about Jesus. I seemed to hear Mum repeating 'He's alive and real today and we can know him...his Presence is real to us' and a very uncomfortable thought came to mind. I shrugged it off. It came back. I felt annoyed. It was the same sort of thought I'd had at the youth club yesterday after Bob had talked about people who didn't know Jesus as their own personal Saviour and Friend.

Don't be silly! I said to the thought. I know all about Jesus. I've been going to church and youth club and Christian Union for years!

Yet the uneasy thought remained: you don't know him like your mum does. You don't know him like Bob does.

This wasn't the sort of thought I wanted to have right now.

"For goodness' sake!" I said out loud, and then flushed scarlet because the others were looking at me. "Sorry," I mumbled. Kendra sniggered, Aunty Ann sniffed and Mum frowned. The embarrassment I felt dispersed my agitated thoughts.

Aunty Ann didn't seem to know how to continue the conversation after that, and said, "Katy! You have a closed mind!" Then Mum went to do the washing-up, clattering the plates loudly.

And I sat back in my chair, unwrapped a piece of gum, and wondered what on earth sort of a weekend we were going to have.

My Dear Relatives

There was an argument going on when I went downstairs for breakfast.

Well, it wasn't so much an argument, but the sort of very controlled disagreement adults have when they want their own way and the other person doesn't agree with them, and they really want to shout and stamp their feet but think that would be undignified.

It was a sunny morning, and very warm for September. Mum was saying we really ought to make the most of the day, and on this point, my aunt agreed with her. But they couldn't decide where to go. Aunty Ann wanted to go to the beach but the nearest one, Wilmington-on-Sea, was what Mum called 'a bit tacky' with piers and candyfloss and amusements - which I liked. Mum said that if they were going to the seaside, why not visit a nice, quiet little fishing village which was only twenty or so miles away - they had a nice museum? Aunty Ann rolled her eyes and said she didn't fancy travelling too far after the journey yesterday - at which point Mum promptly said it was even further to Wilmingham-on-Sea. So they finished up agreeing to go somewhere else.

That's how we ended up at the Millstead District Working Railway.

We piled into Aunty Ann's ancient car. I was squashed in between Dorian and Kendra, who was wearing the shortest pair of short shorts I'd ever seen - when my mum had clapped eyes on them, she'd breathed in very sharply and asked if Kendra was going to change before we went. She didn't.

"Coo," said Kendra, "Stuck in the back of the car with these two spotty blimps!" And before I could say anything to that, she went on, "What a horrid day it's going to be, what with that Mrs Kettle cooking bacon and eggs - bacon! And Dorry eating it - "

"Stop moaning, darling, you know Dorian is an Unenlightened Soul," said my aunt.

Dorian didn't say anything in his defence. But then, he never did say much. I wondered what Unenlightened Soul meant. It sounded awful, so I offered Dorian some chewing-gum, which he accepted with a smile.

The Millstead District Working Railway actually wasn't a working railway at all. Or at least, it didn't work much. A handful of people who liked old steam trains had bought some land and set about making it into an old-fashioned railway which they opened at weekends and for parties of schoolkids. They'd laid a short length of track, and completed the project with floral-covered station, footbridge and signal box.

I found it dull, but Mum liked anything that smacked of the olden days. Aunty Ann glanced about with glazed eyes as the sun got hotter, and Kendra yawned and said how far away was the beach. But Dorian seemed to snap out of his usual stupor, saying, "Cool!" as he stared at the huge old steam engines.

Kendra and I finished up on the nobbly grey footbridge looking down the track, watching the signals going up and down and bits of track switching about as Dorian learned how to use the gadgets in the signal box. He looked really happy for once and waved to us. Kendra said, "Sad, isn't it?", and I said, "No," and turning round, spied Mum dragging Aunty Ann along a platform towards a reconstructed station building. "Mum loves it here."

"Well, she would. It's like walking back into the 1950s."

"What's that meant to mean?"

Kendra looked at me, witheringly. "Well, she's a bit - you know. Old-fashioned."

That was true, of course. But I wasn't going to have Kendra criticising my mum.

"Hmm. At least she doesn't harp on and on about a load of trash like your mum does! Negative energies and daft diets and silly souls!"

"How dare you! My mum's profound!"

"Profound? What's that mean? She keeps rabbiting on and on about so-called spiritual rubbish?"

"You've got a nerve. Your mum's just the same."

"She's not!"

Kendra's eyes narrowed, vindictively. "Your mum's the sort of person who thinks she's always right and everyone else is wrong. She's always trying to get Jesus and church into the conversation. Even last night. When we used to stay over with you when we were kids she was always trying to get us interested in the Bible and we used to have to say our prayers and go to church and Bible Class and stuff!" Kendra smirked. "You don't still have to do all that stuff, do you?"

"I don't *have* to."

"You do, though, don't you?"

"I'm a Christian," I declared, trying to dismiss

any of the doubts I'd begun to feel on the subject.

"Only 'cos your mum says you have to be. I bet you've never even had a single thought of your own about religion. Mum says we ought to find our own paths. She'd never ever force me or Dorry to do anything we didn't want to do."

"Mum doesn't force me to do anything!"

"Oh, yeah. You always do what your mum wants," Kendra sneered, "I'll bet you're only a so-called Christian because she wants you to be. I bet you haven't got faith in anything really."

"I have. I do believe in Jesus. I do."

"Yeah? You don't sound so sure. Anyway, if you do, it's only because your mum tells you to. You'd probably believe in flying saucers if your mum said they were real. You haven't got an original thought in your head. Have you?"

"I really hate you, Kendra!"

"Hmm. Looks like I've hit a sore spot! Sore spot! Hah hah! That's a good one - your face is full of sore spots!" She looked down her rather large nose at me, and walked off. I stood there, watching her go down the steps and along the platform. She turned round and stuck her tongue out at me. I felt furious with her; furious, and shaken. She really had hit a 'sore spot', after all. I wished Kendra and her rotten family would go home.

I trailed after my cousin, and watched Dorian skipping across the track, more animated than I'd ever seen him. Mum and Aunty Ann were in the old station building looking at a mock-up of a typical olde worlde station master's office. My aunt looked bored stiff.

"Shall we go and have lunch in the restaurant

47

car?" Mum suggested.

"No, darling, no thanks," Aunty Ann shot back.

"Oh," said Dorian, "I'd really like - "

"Shut up, darling," said my aunt.

"There's a lovely priory about five miles away," said Mum, "Mostly old ruins, but the nuns - "

"Actually, I've got rather a headache," said Aunty Ann.

And that was the end of our day out.

We went home, and the atmosphere in the car wasn't very happy, not least because the back windows didn't open and it was stifling. It got hotter and hotter and stickier and stickier in the car. I felt so sick I forgot to feel angry and upset, and I was tremendously relieved when we turned into Wingold Way at last, pulling up at number 2.

"Fresh air!" I exclaimed, trying to get out of the car.

"Oi!" said Dorian, as I tripped over his long legs and staggered onto the pavement. Then, a strong hand appeared, caught me and prevented me from falling.

"Oops! Careful, there!"

Bleached Hair was smiling as he let me go.

"Oh!" I said, and he winked at me, and walked up his front drive. Des, the other lodger, was fiddling about under the bonnet of his van, and Bleached Hair stopped to chat to him. I felt completely blown away. Oh wow! He'd spoken to me again! He'd touched me! He'd noticed me! Well, he could hardly not, really, considering I almost fell in a heap at his feet. But still; I felt I was floating on clouds. With great satisfaction, I noticed Kendra's jealous stare.

"Samantha, you really are clumsy," Mum said,

48

as we went indoors, "I suppose that was another of our new neighbours. At least he didn't tell you off for almost falling on him."

"Tell me off!" As if I were some child! I felt offended. But then I thought of how it must have seemed to Bleached Hair - a spotty kid lolling about all over the pavement - I felt myself blush and my delight turned to sudden gloom. It was no good. I'd have to do something to really impress him with my looks and wit and charm. Only I didn't know what or how.

I don't know if Mum felt a bit guilty that my dear relatives - or at least Ann and Kendra - hadn't enjoyed the morning, so she offered to heat up some WOOF diet-friendly pizzas for lunch, and Aunty Ann cheered up a little, and said maybe if she could sit in the garden her headache would disappear. Dorian and Kendra helped her get some old canvas chairs and a sun lounger out of the shed, and Ann said she'd put something more comfortable on instead of the long floaty frock she was wearing, and went upstairs. She came down again wearing something equally floaty but I didn't take much notice - I was too busy giving Mum a hand with the pizzas, which really did look and smell delicious.

"It's so lovely and warm today," she said, "We may as well eat them in the garden."

We carried the pizzas out on trays. It was then we saw what my aunt was doing.

"Oh!" said my mum.

Aunty Ann was wearing just a bikini, the floaty wrap draped over the back of the sun lounger. There was quite a lot of my aunt in places and not much of

49

the bikini. She was lying there, soaking up the sun, whilst Kendra sat demurely by. Dorian was still poking about in the shed.

"Oh, my goodness!" mumbled Mum, "What will the neighbours say?"

"Oh!" I said, imagining that gorgeous boy from next door getting an eyeful of my aunt. How totally embarrassing!

"Coo-ee!" cried Aunty Ann, shielding her eyes from the sun, "Pizzas ready, darling?"

"Sunbathing, Ann? In September?" Mum managed a thin smile.

"A glorious last burst of summer sunshine! Got to take advantage of it! Come on, Katy. Surely you've got a bikini, too? Whip it on, darling."

The notion of my mum whipping on a bikini made me blink. My mum's idea of stripping off in summer was a flowery skirt and a short sleeved blouse. I cast a nervous glance at next door's windows. But before I could get too worried about what Bleached Hair would think, there was a cry from the shed, and the sound of something falling on Dorian.

"Oh! My baby!" shrieked Aunty Ann, leaping out of the sun lounger, "Darling! Mummy's here!"

By the time my frantic aunt, Mum, and I had extricated the squashed boy from an old bike, a piece of rotten timber, and some large cobwebs, the pizzas were cold, and Kendra had disappeared. Fortunately, Dorian had suffered nothing more serious than a bruised leg and a cut on his hand, but my aunt made such a fuss you would think he'd broken his neck. She kept wittering on about air ambulances and doctors and kept kissing his forehead - which I didn't think he much liked.

"Oh! Dorry! If anything ghastly had happened to you, darling, I couldn't have coped! Where's Kendra? Where's Kendra?" my aunt cried.

"Go and find your cousin, Samantha," said Mum, quietly.

She wasn't in the kitchen. I went into the hall, and it was then that I realised the front door was wide open. Kendra was standing by our front gate - talking to Bleached Hair!

He was smiling at her, and nodding, and she was smiling too, and I noticed how very long and brown her legs looked in those short shorts! Before I had time to feel stunned or angry or envious, Bleached Hair said something to her, then said, "See you later!" to Des, who was still working on his van, and walked off down the road. Kendra spotted me, and came in, looking smug.

"Wow, your neighbour's nice. Really nice. What's the matter, Sam? You're red in the face. You don't fancy him, do you?" she sniggered, as I slammed the front door, "Bit old for you. He's nineteen. I bet you don't even know his name. He's called Luce."

I spluttered something unintelligible.

"Honestly, you do, don't you? You fancy him! You silly kid. As if a boy like that would ever give you a second glance!" Kendra's lip curled. "He was telling me all about the night-life here in this miserable little town. I suppose I could've asked you about all the details of the clubs and pubs, you're bound to know!" And she laughed, sarcastically.

"Well, I don't know why you want to know about them, anyway," I snapped, "You're going home tomorrow - and I hope you never come back!"

"What, poor little Sammy's scared I'm going to go to The Black Dog and get off with Luce?" Kendra pulled a face, "Dunno why. Somebody's going to, he's gorgeous - and it won't be you!"

"Why don't you shut up?"

"I told you you weren't really a Christian. Christians don't tell people to shut up. You're a little hypocrite. A spotty little hypocrite."

"If you don't shut up - "

"Kendra!" Aunty Ann was in the hall, now, looking wild-eyed, "Where have you been? Didn't you know your brother's just had the most frightful accident?"

"I'm OK," said Dorian's voice from the kitchen.

"He could've been killed!" declared my aunt, melodramatically, "That shed's a death trap!"

"I don't think it really is," said Mum, "Dorian was poking around, and - "

"And where were you, when you were needed?" Aunty Ann shouted at Kendra, "Your aunt Katy and your cousin helped rescue him. And what did you do? You vanished!"

Kendra looked sullen. "I was hot, so I came in. I opened the front door to let some air in."

Hah! I thought, fuming. Got out of the way of any lifting and shoving, and then opened the front door once she saw Bleached Hair - Luce - was out there! Luce! I started to think about that unusual name. What was it short for? Lucy? Surely not! I was so preoccupied with that thought, I missed how everything blazed out of control. But soon, my aunt was hysterical, screeching about her Useless Offspring, and

Kendra was gazing at her with tight-lipped resentment.

To my horror, Aunty Ann burst into tears. Kendra rushed out of the house and across the road to Mrs Kettle's. Aunty Ann collapsed on the sofa, and Mum put her arm round her sister, and my aunt sobbed that no-one loved her. I stared at her - I wasn't used to seeing adults crumble and cry like this. The only time I'd ever seen my mum cry was when I was six and she told me Dad wouldn't be coming home, and we'd have to trust Jesus to take care of us. Even then, she didn't sob. Her cheeks were just wet.

Mum motioned me to leave the two of them alone, and I did. I wandered out into the garden. Dorian was there, kicking at the gravel path.

"She's never really been happy since Dad left," he said, gruffly, "It's like a rollercoaster ride, living with Mum."

"I'm sorry," I said.

He shrugged, and went indoors. And I felt grateful that although my mum had had to manage without my dad for years and years, she'd never once fallen apart so dreadfully like I'd seen my aunt do today. I couldn't help but wonder if that had something to do with the fact that she really believed that Jesus was with us - my aunt didn't have Jesus.

We didn't see Aunty Ann again until dinner time. She and my mum spent most of the afternoon upstairs in the little office, talking in low voices. Kendra kept out of the way, returning later on to find out how her mum was. The evening meal was a very subdued affair, with Aunty Ann all red-eyed, and my cousins very quiet.

They went home the next day at ten o'clock so

we missed church that morning.

As Dorian put their cases in the car, Mum gave Ann a hug and said she'd pray for her. And instead of saying "Narrow!" my aunt just gave a watery smile. Then Mrs Kettle, who was there to say goodbye to them, said how much she'd miss dear Dorian. Kendra sneered at me as she got in the car - but I couldn't feel cross with her anymore, I just felt incredibly sorry she had a mum like Aunty Ann.

I was also very pleased that she was going and couldn't get her hands on Luce.

The Black Dog

I sat up, suddenly.

It was dark. The luminous figures on my bedside clock read 3:10. I'd been having a horrible dream - Kendra's patronising face had featured heavily in it.

I lay down again. I had to get some sleep - it was school in the morning. But when I shut my eyes I seemed to see Kendra again, smirking at me. I wouldn't want to be her in a million years, but oh, I did wish I looked like she did; all smooth skin and tanned legs. Still, I remembered, Luce had spoken to me as well as to my cousin. Oh, if only I could just spend some time really talking to him, getting to know him, instead of just tripping over him! I drifted off to sleep again, but woke up at seven with exactly the same thoughts whirring round.

"What's the matter with you?" asked Amanda, later, as we ate our lunches.

"Eh?"

"You've hardly touched your lasagne. You love lasagne. Not sick, are you?"

No, I wasn't sick. I was just thinking. Amanda looked fantasic, even in the deadly dull bottle green school uniform we had to wear. I'd started to wonder why I was the only ugly duckling in the whole world, especially when the doll-like Debi Daley made her way over to our table and plonked herself down.

"Hiya," Debi twinkled at Amanda. "How's Tank? Not having lunch with him today?"

"No, poor baby, he's off with a cold."

"Thank goodness," I muttered. I was fed up with having to share my friend with Tank Willis.

I picked at my lasagne whilst Debi delicately nibbled her salad leaves and Amanda scraped out her yoghurt pot.

"Oh dear," said Debi, "English next lesson. I really hate English. Don't you, Amanda?"

"No, not really. I don't much like that book we're reading, though."

"It's pretty boring," I agreed, "But it's not so bad when you get into it."

Debi sighed. "It's all right for you two. You really understand all that stuff."

"What stuff?" asked Amanda.

"Everything." Debi pushed out her lower lip and for a moment didn't look quite so cute. "I dunno. I wish I had brains."

"You have got brains, Debi," said Amanda, kindly - and not particularly truthfully.

"Yes, but they don't work like yours do." A tragic expression crossed the porcelain brow. "I suppose you'll both go to college and get great jobs. Do you ever think about what you're going to do when you're older?"

"Sometimes," I said.

Debi gazed at me with her huge blue eyes. "You're clever, Sammy. Aren't you?"

"Not really." For the first time ever I was beginning to feel a little warmth for the vacuous Debi. Maybe she wasn't quite so shallow and unfeeling as I'd always thought. Perhaps she lay awake at 3:10 in the morning worrying about how dense she was.

"Don't be modest, Sammy," said Amanda, loyally, "Debi, she's going to be a teacher."

Debi's face lit up. "Oh yes! Then she'll make a lot of money and she can do something about her looks!"

"What!" I felt like biting Debi Daley. But she hadn't meant it maliciously. She went on, trying to be helpful.

"Don't worry, Sammy. Some boys like girls who aren't very pretty. Don't they, Amanda? But of course, there's that other thing with you, Sammy. That's a problem."

"What other thing?" I asked, astounded.

"You're religious, aren't you? I mean, that's very likely to put boys off, even if you ever got one interested. They wouldn't want all that churchy stuff. Isn't that likely to put them off, Amanda?"

Amanda shrugged. "Well, I don't know. I suppose so."

"Boys don't want to hear all that Bible stuff. Do they, Amanda? I mean, you don't want people thinking - look, what I mean is, we know you, but boys might think you were a bit weird."

"I know boys, lots of boys!" I protested, "They don't think I'm weird!"

The others looked at me.

"They don't!" I said. "I'm not!"

Debi smiled, sympathetically. "We're talking about boys that you could go out with. Attractive boys. Not just the silly kids in our class. I mean, like, really cool boys. Boys like that might think this church stuff is a bit - er - childish, I suppose. Having a girlfriend who goes to Sunday School or whatever, isn't exactly cool, is it?"

"I don't go to - "

"I know!" Debi slapped her small palm on the table. "Why don't you both come round to my house and we could do something with Sammy's face and hair. Then she might get a boyfriend!"

"I don't think Sammy's really interested in boys," said Amanda, glancing at me and seeing I was about to explode with wrath and do something drastic to Debi Daley.

"Oh," said Debi, batting her eyelashes at me, "Oh well, that's probably her hormones or something. Don't worry, Sammy. My sister - the one who's a beautician - says people mature at different rates. She said - "

Now my temper flared. I really had had enough of being talked about by people and family members as if I were six years old. "I do like boys! And what's more - oh, never mind."

Debi stared. "Do you fancy someone, Sammy? Who? What class is he in?"

"Oh, he doesn't go to this school," I said, "Or any school. He's nineteen, actually. And really gorgeous. And what's more," I added, with more conviction than I really felt, "he likes me, too."

Amanda smiled slightly. "Sammy. Come on. You're making it up."

"Amanda! You think I'm lying?"

My best friend looked a bit awkward. "Well, no, but - come on, Sammy. There's no need to - "

"You don't believe me!" I sat back in astonishment. "Why not? Because you think I'm - what's the word - 'immature'? You do, don't you?

Well, I'm not. And I can look as cool as any of you, too. I really am fed up with you lot thinking I'm a kid."

Amanda didn't look convinced. She glanced at Debi with a 'I'd like to see this nineteen year old gorgeous boy!' expression on her face. She thought he was a figment of my imagination! For a moment, she looked as condescending as my cousin Kendra, and I felt really cross with her.

"If you must know, he's my new next-door neighbour. And what's more, I know where he goes in the evening, so if you want to see him, just go to The Black Dog!"

"When?" said Debi, excitedly.

"What?"

"When? When're you going? Oh!" She clapped her hands together. "How marvellous! You're going to a pub! You'll have to really dress up to make yourselves look older so they'll let you in."

"Eh?" I said.

Amanda started laughing. "Sammy, you should see your face. You look horrified! Debi, can you really see Sammy going into a pub? Her mum would have twenty purple fits!"

"What's my mum got to do with it?" I snapped, "I've got a mind of my own, you know!"

"I'm sorry, Sammy. It's just - you - and a pub - and the thought of what your mum would say!"

"All right!" I said, as they kept tittering, "All right, Amanda, we jolly well will go! Tonight! I'll be round for you at seven, so you'd better be ready!"

"Oh!" exclaimed Debi, "Cool! Totally, totally cool!"

I didn't feel totally cool when I was lying to Mum about why I was going to Amanda's that evening.

"It's - er - this geography project," I mumbled, hating myself for telling a fib but knowing perfectly well that Mum would never ever let me out of the house if she thought I was going anywhere near a pub. But she seemed concerned about something else - Mr Upson wasn't very well - and she agreed surprisingly easily. She walked me half-way to Amanda's house on her way to visit the old man, and made me promise to get Amanda's mum to bring me home which I agreed to do, and felt even more awful because I knew that Amanda's mum and dad were out on Tuesdays. I wasn't much like a 'saintly child' right now, was I?

My heart was pounding as I walked to Amanda's. What on earth was I doing? Going to a pub! I was only thirteen! I'd never in my life before ever wanted to go into one. They looked dark and gloomy inside and stank of stale alcohol, and when Amanda's parents rolled home from an evening in one, she said they argued horribly, and were miserable all the next day. And she'd been right that my mum would go mad if she knew what I planned to do. She loathed pubs.

Then I remembered 'Young for her age!' and 'Plays with dolls!', Kendra's sneering face, and Amanda and Debi who thought I was unattractive and immature. I imagined a scenario where I walked into the pub and Luce was there and paid me some attention. Amanda would be stunned - Debi would hear about it and she'd shut up, too - and most of all, I'd feel grown-up at last. Because pubs were definitely for grown-ups, weren't they?

I even tried telling myself - not particularly successfully - that they had a certain adult glamour, in a dubious, murky sort of way.

Amanda's house was a neat semi-detached with lots of African marigolds in the front garden. I rang the bell, she opened the door, and we went upstairs to her bedroom, where I put down my canvas bag which Mum had thought was full of books, but in fact held my smart jeans, and best top.

"I can't quite believe we're doing this," Amanda said, shutting the door behind her.

"Oh?" I fiddled around in my bag and found the black eyeliner and lipstick.

Amanda sat down abruptly on her frilly duvet. "I'm really surprised at you!"

"Why? Because you've found out I wear make-up too? Why shouldn't I? Everybody else does!"

"But your mum - "

"Will you shut up about my mum? What about your mum? I don't suppose she'd be too happy, or your dad, if they knew where we were going! So what?"

She frowned. "Sammy, what's happened to you?"

"I've changed. The old Sammy's gone!"

Amanda blinked. "Does your mum know?"

I ignored her. "Have you got a mirror?"

She gave me a small hand-held one, and I carefully applied some eyeliner and not too much lipstick. Amanda was wearing mascara and some blusher. She silently handed them over to me, and I'd watched her often enough to know how to put both on. I thought I'd done it quite well, and when Amanda said, "Oh!", I knew I must look quite different to the usual old Samantha.

I pulled on my smart jeans, and Amanda put on a pair of tight black trousers and a spangly crop top. Then she sat on her bed again and bit her lip and tossed her loose hair about.

"Look, Sammy. I don't know if you're trying to prove something, but you don't have to. I'm your friend. I know I've been going on about Tank and I've been ignoring you. I was just so pleased to have a nice boy ask me out. I suppose I might have made you feel a bit bad about all that. I'm sorry. I didn't mean to."

"You're getting cold feet about going to the pub!"

"No I'm not!"

I could see she was. I certainly was. But I wasn't going to back out of the idea now - I wasn't going to have her crowing at school that poor Sammy was afraid, and couldn't go through with it - probably because she was too frightened of what would happen if her mum found out!

The thought of my mum finding out made my stomach lurch. But she wouldn't. Nobody she knew went to pubs. And Luce - if he was there - wouldn't tell her...would he? I'd have to ask him not to. The very thought of him gave me renewed courage. What if he was there, and talked to me, maybe even asked me out for a date! What would Amanda think then!

I unwrapped some gum. "OK. Let's go!"

I marched out of her bedroom, and down the stairs. We went outside, and soon we were staring at The Black Dog. It was an olde worlde building with leaded light windows. Fading petunias in hanging baskets hung from the white walls, and the sign - a black Labrador sniffing the air as if he were about to flush out a pheasant - creaked slightly in the evening breeze. A florid face stared out the window at us, and I jumped.

I had a sudden thought. What if Luce wasn't in there? Kendra hadn't exactly said what nights he went in. I had just presumed, somehow, that it was every night. What kind of drink would I order? What would we do when we got in there? I glanced about. In the twilight, I could have sworn I saw Mrs Kettle across the road. I could just see her rushing over, shocked at my appearance and that I was going into a pub, and racing off to tell my mum, who would be horrified, and dreadfully hurt, and - but no, it wasn't Mrs Kettle, just someone who looked like her.

"If you want to change your mind," Amanda whispered, "I'll understand."

The pub door was half open. The blackness of the inside was broken only by a flash of red and yellow as someone played a gaudy fruit machine which promised Double Money. There was that sickening smell of alcohol. It was horrible.

A big man came to the door. He had a huge gut and I realised it was his red-cheeked face that had peered at us out of the window. I felt scared. I didn't like the look of him at all.

"'Ere, youse two," he said, "I 'opes you don't think you're comin' in."

I noticed one or two figures in the darkness of The Black Dog.

The big man put his hands on his hips. "I ain't gonna lose my licence. Come back when you're eighteen and not before!"

Some men at the bar laughed and I felt as small as an ant.

"We weren't coming in anyway!" said Amanda, and the big man said, "Huh! See youse don't!" and slammed the door.

Somebody was coming along the pavement. Before I had time to think about what had just happened, I heard a very familiar voice.

"Hi!"

Luce!

He smiled. "I didn't recognise you for a minute. You look different."

"Oh," I said. He was so close I could see the colour of his eyes - light blue. I wished I could think of something cool to say.

"You look like you're ready for a night out. Never seen you in The Dog, have I?"

"Er - no!" He obviously thought I was older than I was!

He yawned. "Oh, excuse me. Late night at college tonight. Missed the bus. I'm tired out." He smiled again. "I don't know your name. I think I should, considering we're neighbours, and I keep bumping into you!"

"Sam," Oh, why did I sound so breathless! "Samantha. It's Samantha."

"You can call me Luce. I think I was talking to your cousin the other day, wasn't I?"

"Um - yeah."

He looked at me. "You really do look different tonight. Have a nice time, girls, wherever you're going or whatever you're doing. You look great, both of you.

See you again, Samantha."

And off he went!

I came back down to planet earth and turned to my gaping friend.

"Wow!" she said, "He was -"

"The boy I told you about that you didn't believe in!"

"Oh!"

The smug expression that had become more and more a frequent visitor to Amanda's features since she started going out with Tank had disappeared.

And I was glad.

Cool

It had never happened before - I was popular.

Debi Daley was sitting opposite me, slightly slack-jawed. Several other girls from my class - girls who normally didn't take much notice of me - were crowded round my desk, eyes wide with admiration. Amanda was enjoying being the joint centre of attention, and seemed a lot more confident telling the others about our adventure than she had actually been when taking part in it. However, she did tend to embellish the tale. I wished she wouldn't.

"Wow!" said one of the listening girls, "This is unreal. Amanda and Sammy being slung out of a pub!"

"Cool!" said someone else, impressed.

I felt a bit uncomfortable at this over-dramatisation of the truth.

"Well, we weren't really slung out, we didn't even - "

Amanda interrupted me. "It was all Sammy's idea. She was meeting a boy there. I'm dead glad I encouraged her to go for it."

"You encouraged me!" I gasped, remembering her reluctance yesterday.

"Everyone, this boy was really fantastic. Blond, tall, and good looking."

"Amanda!" I said, "I wasn't exactly meeting ..."

"Shh!" she whispered to me, "This is your chance to really look cool in front of the others. I'm helping you here."

"This wonder boy looks a bit like Lennie from The View, does he?" said a girl called Trina Finch who knew what I thought of The View, and who had never liked me very much. And I was so irritated by that comment I didn't stop Amanda from tossing her hair and saying, "Don't be daft. He's much better looking. And he practically asked her out. He's nineteen!"

"Nineteen!" said Trina Finch.

"Sammy, I didn't think you had it in you!" Debi patted my arm.

"Neither did I," mumbled Trina Finch, "Maybe I was wrong about her."

Debi nodded. "I think we were all wrong about this girl. Sammy, we all thought you were a bit wet, to tell the honest truth, but well, that's just not true anymore, is it?"

I sat back in my seat, unsure of how to take this back-handed compliment, as she continued.

"There's no stopping her now! The new Sammy's going to be a lot more fun than the old one!"

"Well, Sammy!" Trina Finch stood up, looking tough and masculine in bottle green trousers. "You've changed. You're different. You used to be really - I dunno."

"Wet!" offered Debi, helpfully, "Wet and boring and all religious and a bit weird."

"Wha - " I began.

"Yeah, that's it," said Trina. She was a big girl with no imagination except when she thought she was being insulted, at which point she'd challenge the offender to a fight. "Huh! She's really one of us now!" She was smiling at me - a brutal, hard little half-smile

- and I didn't much like it. She'd never smiled at me before, not once, and I wasn't completely sure I wanted to be 'one of us' with her.

The bell for first lesson sounded.

"You're cool, Sammy!" said Debi, "You and Amanda both are!"

Amanda simpered a bit and looked pleased with herself - and maybe pleased to have a friend who was at last considered 'cool'. She didn't look quite so happy when the teacher asked her to tell the class all about French Verbs. I listened to her struggling through the verbs, and thought how very pleasant it was to be looked at with admiration for a change. The story escalated all morning, and by lunch, everyone knew that Sammy had an older boyfriend, and I'm sorry to say I didn't deny it. OK, so it wasn't exactly true. But I did have an older boy interested in me - sort of - and it was really something to be thought of as someone who could attract a handsome partner rather than just Sammy who went to church with her mum and had spots. I was beginning to feel grown-up at last and walked tall down the corridor between Debi and Amanda, feeling their equal rather than just the dreary girl who tagged along whilst they talked about boys - until a pale-faced eleven year old with thin legs raced up to me and brought me back down to earth. It was Drippy Dinah who went to the youth club.

"Hello, Sammy!" she said, with a shy smile, "Are you coming to C.U.?"

"What's C.U.?" asked Debi, blankly.

"Christian Union," said the kid.

Debi screwed her small nose up. I could see she thought it deeply Uncool to go to Christian Union. A thought struck me. If I went to the Union meeting, would it mean that my popularity would slide down to position nil again? I'd only had a brief morning of being cool - I didn't want it all to be over by the afternoon! I couldn't risk it.

"Sorry, Dinah," I said, "I can't come today."

The kid looked disappointed. I felt a bit bad - I quite liked little Dinah. Besides, not many kids went to the fortnightly C.U. meetings, just a few young ones, and a fourteen-year-old boy who wasn't sure whether he wanted to be a vicar or an archaeologist when he left school, so made sure he went to C.U. and the Fossil Club just to hedge his bets. Mrs Foster, who was young and fun and taught R.E., ran the C.U. and I knew she was worried that the numbers were dwindling. I felt I'd let her down if I didn't go. But I wasn't the old Sammy any more. I'd changed. And I liked being different and meant to keep it up.

Besides, I really didn't want to go to a meeting that might revive any of the uneasy feelings I'd been experiencing lately about just where I stood with Jesus - feelings I'd been trying to squash down and forget about because I didn't want them intruding on my new life. Especially not now. So I repeated, "Sorry, Dinah," and pushed past her.

"Oh, well done," said Debi's voice in my ear, "You don't want to hang out with little kids, do you, Sammy?"

"No!" I said, fervently, thinking of my mum's words - 'young for her age'!

"Samantha!"

Mrs Foster was clip-clopping towards us on high heels, holding a pile of books, a big smile on her friendly face. She dumped the books into my arms, and opened the door to the R.E. room, which we were just passing.

"Oh, Mrs Foster," I began, "I'm sorry, I'm not..."

"I think we'll have a small number today," she said, brightly, "There are so many colds about! But never mind. I've got such a lovely story to tell you about a dear Christian lady I know who has been so ill and do you know, our Lord Jesus has been so real to her!"

Debi coughed, loudly.

"Hold on a moment!" I said to my friends. I walked into the R.E. room, and put the books on the nearest table. "Mrs Foster!"

"Yes, Samantha?" she was crouched on the floor, rummaging about in a cupboard, "Oh! Where is that book - 'True Stories, Changed Lives' - don't suppose you've seen it, have you, Samantha? A big book with a white dove on the front?"

"No." I took a deep breath. "Mrs Foster, I'm - "

"Samantha, sorry to interrupt, but we're going to be talking about the importance of testimonies today." Mrs Foster looked up at me, "Could you put some paper and pens out on the desks?"

I saw Dinah hovering by the door. It occurred to me that she was one person who had always looked at me with admiration, for some reason I never quite fathomed.

"What's a testimony, Mrs Foster?" asked Dinah.

"Well, in this context, it's being able to tell other people something about what Jesus has done for us in our own lives. A personal witness. It can help and encourage us when we speak like this, and help others come to know him, too."

"Oh!" said Dinah, excitedly, "Can I give my testimony, Mrs Foster? How I came to ask Jesus into my life?"

"Of course you can, Dinah!" smiled Mrs Foster, "Oh - I do wish I could find 'True Stories, Changed Lives'!"

My friends appeared behind Dinah, and Debi mouthed, "Come on!"

"Mrs Foster," I said, determined.

"Yes? Oh dear! Where is that book? Aha!"

"Mrs Foster, I'm sorry, but I can't come to C.U. today."

There! I'd said it. I stared at her, defiantly. She couldn't make me stay! If she tried, I'd tell her I jolly well didn't want to come anymore. And I didn't. Did I?

But she didn't try to make me. She just looked terribly sad. I could hardly bear it. I nearly said I'd stay after all. "Oh! I'm sorry about that." She stood up, clutching a large book. "Any particular reason, Samantha?"

I looked at my friends. Mrs Foster saw them, too.

"Oh. I see."

"I'm sorry," I said. And I actually really did mean it.

"Oh, Sammy!" said Dinah, "I was hoping to hear you give your testimony, too, about how you met Jesus, and what he's done in your life!"

I stared at her with the shock of realisation that I honestly wouldn't know what to say.

Mrs Foster was talking again. "We'll miss you, Samantha. But I can't force you to come to C.U. if you don't want to. Still, you know you'll be welcome to come next time."

One or two of the other members of C.U. drifted into the classroom.

"Sammy, I wish you'd stay," said Dinah, "My dad says God honours those who honour him. If you come to C.U. it's like honouring him. Isn't it, Mrs - "

At this point, Debi started giggling. She'd heard the kid.

"Well if you're not staying, I'd better shut the door," said Mrs Foster, glancing at Debi, "And make a start."

And the door shut behind me as they started their meeting. I felt strangely excluded. It was silly, because I'd chosen not to stay. That uncomfortable feeling about my own Christianity had intensified with the revelation that I didn't have a personal testimony about how Jesus came into my life. It occurred to me that all I could have said truthfully was that I'd heard a lot about Jesus from other people and that I'd really believed he was real when I was little. But now?

"You know, I'm not really anti-religion, or anything," Debi chattered, "Are you, Amanda? It's just that, well, it's all right for kids, isn't it? But not when you're grown-up...not in real life." She linked her arm through mine, and propelled me down the corridor.

I thought about what she'd said as we went into the library, where we were meant to study, but where we usually read magazines and had a chat at lunch-times. My mind was whizzing and whirring with thousands of unwanted thoughts. Was the reason Jesus had been more believable to me when I was young because I was just a silly little kid in those days? Was he OK for children to believe in, and that was all - like a fairy tale, unreal and fantastical, a bit like Santa Claus - a nice dream, but something to be dumped when you got older and 'real life' kicked in?

An unexpected wave of sickness flooded me. What was I doing, listening to Debi twittering on about something she knew nothing about? Mrs Foster was an adult. Jesus was real to her. She'd often spoken about him in just the same way as Bouncing Bob, and my mum, did. They loved him. Yes, they did. You couldn't love something or someone who wasn't real. Could you?

Then, as Debi opened a magazine she'd brought to school, and showed me a picture of The View, I remembered my crush on Lennie, the lead singer. I really admired Lennie. I'd almost felt as if I loved him, sometimes, but I was wise enough to know that it wasn't real love I felt, just infatuation for an ideal - the ideal boy I imagined he was, kind, good, thoughtful, fun. He probably wasn't anything like that really, at home with his mum and people who knew him.

I suddenly felt as if a hugely deep thought was hanging around in my head and I couldn't quite get a grip of it. I gazed at the picture of The View as Debi's chattering washed over me like tepid water. I was only half aware of Amanda's comments, which sounded weary and increasingly bored.

Lennie from The View was alive. He was real, but I didn't know him personally. Other people did. But I didn't. If I met him and knew him, I could maybe love him, truly. But until I actually did meet him, all I'd ever know about him was what other people wrote about him, said about him, or portrayed him as on TV...was it a bit like that with Jesus?

My heart started thumping. All the thoughts and doubts that had been bugging me lately crystallised into reality in one amazing moment. Right then I saw it clearly and wondered why I'd never quite grasped it before.

You had to really really meet Jesus yourself to truly know him! That was the difference between me and Bob and mum and Mrs Foster and even Dinah, and everyone else I knew who talked about him as if he were real. I might know all about him, but I'd never really met him. I might have believed what my mum and others said about him when I was small, but I'd never asked him into my life as - what had Bob said?- my personal Saviour and Friend. I knew right then without the shadow of a doubt that there was a deeper level of belief, something I hadn't actually experienced for myself, but which was there, and available, if only I wanted it.

It was as if someone switched a light on and I breathed in, sharply.

But did I want it?

"Sammy!" Debi was shaking my arm. "Are you OK? You look weird! Did you hear me? Sammy! I said, because Amanda's going out with Tank on Saturday, would you like to go shopping with me instead?"

I stared blankly at her. And she took my rather stupified silence as being a great big yes'.

"I know you were probably flattered she asked

you," said Amanda, later, "because she never has before. But you'll find it much more boring going out with her than going shopping with me!"

I suppose I was far too pre-occupied with other things to take much notice of the fact that Amanda was beginning to feel quite hurt by my increasing popularity with Debi Daley.

Problems

If anyone had told me I was going to have my first real encounter with God in the fridge, I'd never have believed them.

It was raining when I got home from school. The unusually hot September weather had broken, and thunder rumbled as I walked up our drive. I was relieved Luce wasn't likely to be home yet, because I looked just like a drowned rat.

It had been an exhausting day. The maths test just after lunch had dispelled all my thoughts about Jesus and when I'd recovered my brain during Art class, I'd come to a conclusion I felt quite comfortable with: that I didn't want to think about this anymore right now. I didn't want to wonder what would happen if I asked Jesus into my life properly, because I had a weird feeling that rather than sending me back to what I was before I began my new, different life of being grown-up, I was very likely going to charge head first into something which would mean I'd be deeply Uncool for all eternity with everyone at school.

I didn't want the other thoughts that assailed me, either, thoughts such as what if I asked him and nothing happened - he still wasn't real to me? And what if I didn't ask him at all?

No, I decided, right now I just wanted to be cool. I'd put aside those intrusive thoughts, and deal with them at a later date when I was ready for them.

I dripped up to our front door. Mum opened it.

She looked a bit flushed in the face.

"Sam! I've only just come in. I simply had to call on dear old Mr Upson. I'm worried about him, poor love. He's had such a nasty cold." She sneezed and dabbed her nose with a tissue.

"I think you've caught it, Mum. That's what comes of hanging round sick old folk."

She blew her nose. "Poor old Mr Upson. It's not nice to be ill and alone. He's such a dear. He said he's been thinking about you. He's been praying for you all afternoon. He said he really feels as if God wants him just to pray and pray and pray for you."

"What!" My heart hammered against my ribs. Surely Mr Upson didn't know about the dilemma I'd been grappling with! How could he know! "Praying! Why?" I added, defensively, "I'm all right!"

"That's what I told him. I said you were a good little girl and that he ought to pray for others who really needed it."

Good little girl! I remembered how 'saintly' I was supposed to be.

"Mr Upson was insistent. He said he must pray for you if that's what God wanted."

That's when I went to the fridge.

"No!" I yanked open the door, "No, no, no. I'm not thinking about it, God. Not right now! I'll think about it all later. Later!" I bit my lip. I was talking to God. Really and truly. Not just sending lists of demands into vague, impersonal space, but addressing someone real. I was almost overcome by the awesomeness of suddenly realising I felt the reality of God. I grabbed some orange juice and slammed the door shut as if I thought I could just leave God in the

77

ice box.

Mum came into the kitchen muttering about cough medicine and honey and lemon drinks. I tried to get my mind on nice, safe, normal, everyday things. Things that weren't earth shattering or scary or meant anything huge and colossal.

"Mum - I'm going shopping with Debi on Saturday."

"Debi? Who's Debi? A new friend?"

"No. I've known her for ages."

"Have you?" Mum sneezed again. "You've never mentioned her before. Where does she live?"

"The other side of town. We're going to meet in the bus station."

"Well, I don't know. I'd like to meet her before you go charging off round town with her."

"Oh, Mum!" I felt cross with her. "I'm not a child, you know! We're not going to start fires or run away or rob banks or anything!"

"No, of course not, Samantha, I never suggested that."

"Why don't you trust me, then?"

Mum looked taken aback. "I do trust you. Of course I do. I think you're a very sensible girl."

"Well then?"

Mum sneezed several more times, and looked so poorly I felt guilty I'd snapped at her.

"Why don't you go to bed, Mum? I can make some dinner for you."

"No, no. You can't, you've got to do your homework, and then you've got to go out tonight."

"What? Oh - the youth club!" Something dawned on me. Mum being unwell was a perfect excuse not to go to the youth club tonight. I really really didn't want to go because I didn't want anything further stimulating more God thoughts I couldn't - or didn't want to - handle.

And after all, I reminded myself, running about with a load of kids just wasn't part of the new, grown-up me. "Mum, I'll skip the club tonight. It doesn't matter. I'll stay in and look after you."

"Don't be so silly! I've only got a cold."

"It might be the flu. You want to take care of yourself. Go to bed!"

"Hmm," Mum sniffed, "I do feel dreadful. Yes, I will go to bed after dinner. But there's no need at all for you to miss the club. I know how much you love it."

"Well, to be honest, Mum, the children are quite young and - "

"And you love children, you want to be a teacher!" She smiled. "Don't worry, Sam, love. I understand!" and she started to prepare a salad for our evening meal. Then I had an idea and pointed out that she was coughing and sneezing all over my food as well as her own, and didn't she feel bad about that? She did, of course, and without much more persuading, disappeared off to bed. I felt incredible relief as I went to the phone.

I rang Bouncing Bob.

"Sorry," I said, "I can't come tonight. My mum's ill. I'm staying in to look after her!"

I put the phone down before he could talk to me about God.

Mum wasn't pleased when she found out I'd phoned Bob. She wanted me to call him back straight

79

away, but I told her she looked ghastly, I was worried, I'd rather stay home, and she relented and said what a thoughtful daughter I was - which made me feel guilty. But I didn't have long to dwell on it, because a sharp ring! ring! on the doorbell turned out to be Mrs Kettle, all teeth and flashing glasses, asking to borrow something or another, which meant she wanted to come over for a gossip. When she heard Mum was ill she rushed upstairs and began clucking round her and fussing like a demented hen.

"Samantha!" she said, as she came downstairs again, "Now then, I'm going to warm some chicken soup for your mother. Chicken soup is just wonderful for colds. It's full of goodness." She squeezed my arm. "Your mother told me you haven't had anything for your tea. I said, 'I can make the little girl her tea, dear, don't you worry about that!' How do sardines on toast grab you?"

"I'm not a little girl!" I snapped, "And I hate sardines, and I can make myself some tea!"

Mrs Kettle didn't seem to hear my offensive tone. She was rummaging in a cupboard for a saucepan, and before I knew what had happened, she'd served Mum - and me - bowls of creamy chicken soup with brown bread. I ungraciously accepted mine, but was glad I did, because it was very tasty. She insisted on staying the rest of the evening, making cups of tea, flapping about, and generally being very annoying - and very kind, which I didn't appreciate; I wished she'd just go home.

Mum was still snorting and sneezing the next day. She was propped up in bed, trying to do some work, and Mrs Kettle began fussing early saying she should take it easy. I didn't offer to stay to help take care of her because I simply couldn't stand the thought of Mrs Kettle's company all day. But when I got in, Mrs Kettle wasn't there after all. She'd left me a pre-cooked dinner and a note saying it was a Pasta Surprise, her own recipe, and needed heating in the microwave. She also said she'd fed Mum - which sounded like something you'd do to an animal in a zoo - but had a meeting with the amateur dramatic society she couldn't possibly miss. She hoped we'd be all right and had scribbled a phone number in case of emergencies.

I smiled. I'd be all right! I certainly would! I went upstairs, said hello to Mum, asked how she was, said she looked awful, and got her some more tissues; then I ate the Pasta Surprise, the surprise being it was incredibly good, and sprawled in front of the TV, watching a soap opera my mum didn't usually like to watch, but which they always talked about at school. And then the doorbell rang.

"Oh no! Not Mrs Kettle again! I thought she'd gone somewhere tonight!"

I snatched open the front door, ready to tell Mrs Kettle that we were perfectly fine and, in the nicest possible way, ask her to push off. But our visitor wasn't Mrs Kettle.

"Hi, Samantha," said Luce, with one of his charismatic grins.

I pulled my thoughts together as quickly as I could.

"Uh - hello, Luce," I said, hoping to sound casual, and not as if the most exciting thing in the world had just happened to me.

81

"I've got something to ask you."

I felt slightly dizzy and had to hold on to the door. He wasn't going to ask me out, was he?

"Can I use your phone? I know it's a cheek, but ours isn't working, and Des has taken the mobile off somewhere."

"The phone?" I blinked at him before his words sank in. "Oh! The phone!"

"You have got one, I take it?"

"Oh, yeah. Of course. We've got two. One's upstairs in Mum's office. Well, it's the third bedroom really, but she uses it - " I was rambling. I pointed into the living-room, and he came in, wiping his feet on the mat. He brushed past me. He smelled of some tangy aftershave.

I hovered about, not knowing what to do next. Obviously, he didn't want me hanging round whilst he made a call. I sat on the bottom stair, trying to do something about my breathing which was too fast. Should I offer him a cup of tea? A coke? A glass of orange? Was that childish? What was the grown-up thing to do? A marvellous thought struck me. Maybe Luce's phone wasn't really out of order at all. Perhaps he was using that as an excuse to come round and see me!

"Sam! Who's that?" Mum shouted from her sick bed.

"Next door neighbour! Using the phone!"

Her bed creaked. I groaned. I did hope she wasn't going to come downstairs and ruin what might be a perfect moment with Luce. But she didn't come down.

I could hear his voice, low on the phone. I felt

as if I could listen to him talk forever. I wished, wished, wished I was wearing some make-up, and tried to flatten the wilder strands of my hair. Then I heard the receiver being replaced. He appeared in the hallway.

"Thanks for that, Samantha."

I shrugged, trying to be nonchalant. "It's all right. Any time."

He looked as if he was about to say something more, but then he nodded towards the half-open front door.

"You're popular tonight. Is this your boyfriend?"

"Eh? Oh!"

Bouncing Bob was walking down the drive!

"Oh, no!" I mumbled, "Not now!"

"Hello, Sammy! Just came to see how your mum is. We really missed you last night."

Please shut up, Bob! I thought, cringing! Please don't say anything else! Oh! I really didn't want Luce to know I went to something as babyish as a youth club! Especially not a church one!

Luce smiled, and winked at me. "See you, gorgeous."

Gorgeous! He'd called me gorgeous! I nearly died of sheer pleasure. Then, as I glanced at Bob - who was watching Luce walk away - I felt a wave of frustration and anger as it occurred to me that he might have just completely trashed what could have been that start of a wonderful relationship with Luce! For all I knew, Luce might have stayed and chatted, and I might have gone to school on Monday truthfully able to say I had a boyfriend!

"Sammy, are you OK? You look a bit funny."

"I'm not funny. I'm fine. Mum's resting. She's just got a bad cold."

"I - er - came to see if you were all right, too, you know. Dinah was at the club last night, and she was very worried about you. She said you hadn't wanted to be at the C.U. meeting."

For goodness' sake! Couldn't I live my own life without people poking their noses in? I clenched my fists. I'd have to have a word with that Dinah.

Bob smiled, warmly. "Sammy, if something's bothering you, I hope you know you can always talk to me about it. Maybe I can help."

"Help!" I thought of Luce, and a series of pictures flashed through my mind; Luce sitting down, having a glass of orange, asking me out on a date; me going to school on Monday morning telling them I really did have a boyfriend! Oh! I felt so, so angry with Bob! It even occurred to me - irrationally and unfairly - that it was his fault for sparking off all these awkwardly-timed God ideas I'd been having!

"Come on, Sammy. I hope you know I'm your friend. Something's troubling you, isn't it? I can tell."

I glanced up the stairs, and closed the door up a bit so just my face was sticking out and Mum had little chance of hearing what I was about to say. I stared at Bob's kindly face. He was obviously really worried about me. But I didn't feel like being nice to him at all. In fact at that moment the poor unfortunate man was my least favourite person in all the world.

"OK, if you must know, I don't want to come to the club anymore. Everyone seems to think I'm still a kid, but I'm not. I'm grown-up now. The youth club's OK for kids but not when you grow up. All right? And actually I'm pretty sick of being known as a God Botherer, too. Because I'm not and I don't know if I want to be. I haven't - I don't - I mean - " I could hardly think of the right words to say, but I suddenly had the nasty urge to hurt Bob's feelings in a silly attempt at some sort of revenge. So I blurted out, "My aunt says being a Christian is narrow. Maybe there's more to life! And perhaps being a Christian is all right if you're very young or very very old and past it!"

To say Bob looked shocked at my vitriolic words is an understatement. I was shaking. I could hardly believe it was me that had said such appalling things. For a very long minute or two, he said nothing. Then he spoke, in a very quiet voice.

"Well, your aunt certainly has a point. Being a Christian is like walking a very narrow path."

I hadn't expected him to agree. I'd expected - what?

"Jesus said so," Bob continued, "He said there's a broad road and a narrow road. He meant that following him is a difficult path to walk along. It's not easy at all. The broad road - living life without him, doing what you want - seems very nice and easy and attractive to us sometimes. But it isn't so important, the difficulty of travelling, when you realise what the final destination is. The narrow road leads to eternal life. The other one doesn't. And Jesus called himself the gate to the narrow road; the only way to everlasting life." He wiped a hand across his face. "Oh dear. I'm preaching. I can see the last thing you want is a sermon right now. Still, I'm glad you found you could be honest with me. Thanks, Sammy."

He was thanking me, now, for being rude to him!

"Just remember, he died on the cross for you, Sammy. You know, we all really deserve God's punishment for the bad things we've done that have hurt him and others, don't we? But God loves us so much he wanted to save us from that, so he sent his only Son, Jesus, to pay the penalty for us. That's why we call him our Saviour - he saved us from the consequences of our wrong actions. He took the blame so we don't have to. Just ask him, and he'll forgive you and give you a life that's lived in the power of his Spirit. Why don't you ask him to do that for you, Sammy? Because you never have, have you? Seems to me you're at a crossroads. Aren't you? Which way will you go?"

Bob knew I didn't have a personal relationship with Jesus! He knew! A crossroads! Yes, that's exactly how I felt. I gulped. I thought of the girls at school and handsome Luce and Bob talking about the narrow path. Something seemed to whisper in my ear that narrow meant Restricted and Boring, but something else assured me that narrow meant Security, Acceptance and Love, the Presence of a loving God in my life.

I couldn't cope with all this. So I snapped "Goodbye!" and shut the door in Bob's face.

The phone rang just then. My hand trembled as I picked up the telephone receiver. I hoped it would be Amanda trilling on for hours about dull, dreary, completely ordinary old Tank.

Little did I know that the news on the other end of the line would be some of the worst I could ever imagine.

Life Stinks

"Sammy, I'm really sorry for you. Your life truly stinks."

Debi smiled sympathetically and finished off her coke.

We were sat in a very sordid cafe at the bus station. The tables looked as if they needed a good wipe-down with a damp cloth, and the place smelled of onions. It was half full of leather jacketed youths. Debi's eyes kept flashing towards the leather jackets.

Debi was right. My life did stink. I thought about what had happened last night.

Mum hadn't actually looked well enough to take that call the previous evening. But it was Mr Fothergill, from Fothergill and Sons, one of her clients, and she heaved herself out of bed and into her little office. She was in there for ages, speaking occasionally in a low voice. I'd thought it was just business, and went into my bedroom to start my homework. Then she'd opened my door.

"Mum!"

She was whiter than she had been before. She sat down on my bed and quietly told me that Mr Fothergill had said the company were 'dispensing with her services'. Just like that. And because she was only a freelance worker who didn't have a proper contract, that was it. She must've thought I didn't understand, because she said that 'dispensing with her services' meant 'goodbye, Mrs Jones'. And 'goodbye, Mrs

Jones' meant there'd be even less money coming into the household.

"But is it so bad? You've got other clients, Mum," I'd said, trying to be helpful. But even as I spoke, I remembered that Fothergill's were her biggest client, the one who gave her most of the work that paid all our bills; Mum had always said she was blessed to have such regular work from Fothergill's because freelance work was so hard to come by.

I'd felt a horrible sensation of cold dread creep up my body which I tried to dispel by telling myself, and Mum, that she could always get more clients.

"Oh, Sam, I wish it was that easy!" Mum started coughing, and she looked so ill and frail I'd begun to get scared. "Oh! I didn't need this. Not now. Dear Lord!"

"Oh, Mum! Things will work out!" I'd assured her, with more conviction than I felt. Her eyes were wet and glassy, and I knew it wasn't just through the coughing. I'd helped her back to bed, and leaning back against her pillow, she'd suddenly looked very much older.

The next morning, I got ready to go and meet Debi in town. I thought I'd attempt to forget the horrible home situation and go and enjoy myself. But I didn't feel much like having a good time. I felt really miserable. I hadn't slept much, and I had heard Mum tossing and turning all night. And then the phone rang again, and I'd answered it hoping that maybe it was Mr Fothergill with some better news. But it wasn't. It was Aunty Ann.

Mum was downstairs, in her dressing-gown, scuffing around in ancient bedroom slippers and looking even more worried than she had the night before. Soon, she was ensconced on the sofa telling Ann all our troubles. And that's when things got even worse.

"Well, there's some light at the end of the tunnel, Sam!" She put the receiver down, and her face broke into a smile for the first time since she'd heard the bad news. "I spent half of last night praying and praying for some sort of answer! Maybe this is it. I must say, I didn't expect an answer quite so soon. I should have more faith, I think! Oh, Sam! Praise the Lord."

"Eh?"

"Ann had an idea. She said if I can't get more work, why don't you and I re-locate to Kent?"

"What!"

"There's more! She lives in that huge rambling old place, and she's got plenty of room - you and I could share the big back bedroom until I got a good job in an office - there's so much more work in Medchester than in little Millstead! Sam! This could be a blessing in disguise. It could be the start of a whole new life!"

A whole new life! Living with my neurotic aunt and patronising Kendra was absolutely not the sort of changed life I'd been hoping for! And horror of horrors, I'd have to share my own private space - my bedroom - with my mother! Oh! I might as well be a complete baby!

"Stinks," said Debi.

I snapped back into the present. Some old ladies had come into the dismal cafe, and the youths had left.

"I'd hate to move away from Millstead!" Debi stood up. "You'll have to go to a new school. You won't have any friends. Poor you."

I unwrapped some gum.

"It's a shame though," she said, as we stood outside and watched the buses pulling in and out of the station, "You'll have to kiss goodbye to that gorgeous boy, won't you?"

"Oh!"

I hadn't thought of that. Of course! I'd never get a chance with Luce, would I, when he was miles and miles away! Oh no! Just when he was showing an interest in me!

We crossed the road. I unwrapped more gum and chewed furiously, my mind spinning with the unfairness of it all.

And then I heard someone call my name.

Pounding feet sounded along the pavement, and somebody tweaked my elbow.

It was Drippy Dinah.

"Sammy! I can't believe it's you. Thank you, Jesus! I've been thinking about you. I wanted to talk to you about something. I'm so pleased to see you."

I was in no mood to be pleasant to anyone much, let alone this scrawny kid who, I suddenly remembered, had told tales about me to Bouncing Bob.

"Dinah, stop pulling my shirt sleeve."

"Looks like you've got a fan club, Sammy!" remarked Debi, sarkily.

"I don't know why you're nearly fainting with delight," I said to Dinah, with a sneer worthy of my cousin Kendra, "Why're you so amazed to see me? I do live in Millstead, you know!"

"At the moment," muttered Debi, just loud enough for me to hear, and I felt a real surge of injustice and unhappiness.

"Sammy, I wanted to have a word with you, that's all." Dinah blinked at me, obviously a bit nervous at my sharp tone. Her scared expression just made me feel more annoyed, somehow.

"What word's that? Something like, 'Please sir, Sammy's not going to Christian Union anymore, or the youth club, isn't she a naughty little girl'? Something like that, eh, Dinah?"

"Er - no, Sammy. I don't know what you mean. I - I wanted to tell you about something at school, Sammy. I've got a problem. I'm a bit frightened. It's this girl called Tanya. Her mum makes corn dollies for harvest festival and - "

"Corn dollies! What on earth are you drivelling on about!"

Dinah's eyes filled with tears. "Sammy! Why're you cross with me? Have I done something wrong?"

"Oh, for goodness' sake! Just leave me alone, you silly little kid! I've got enough problems of my own without having to listen to yours!"

Debi nodded, approvingly.

"Push off, kid. Sammy doesn't want you hanging round. Child! Come on, Sammy. Shall we go to 'Sounds'?"

I allowed Debi to steer me away from Dinah. We headed for the music shop, and as my anger subsided, I began to feel bad. How horrible I'd been to the kid! But then I remembered that she'd told tales on me. I didn't want to hear her bleating about her stupid little problems - what problems could she ever have, compared to the terrible things that were happening to me? Silly little Dinah! But when we reached 'Sounds', I soon became distracted as I listened to the thumping beat of the music, and started rifling through stacks of interesting CDs; in no time at all I found I was forgetting about Dinah, my mum, Fothergill's, Aunty Ann, my spiritual confusion, and everything else in the world.

The View had just released a new CD. I wanted to show Debi, but glancing round the store, I saw she was talking to a dark-haired boy who was standing behind a counter. I fleetingly thought that if she smiled much more broadly at him her teeth would drop out onto the floor.

Next minute, she was tapping me on the shoulder.

"Let's go."

"What? Now? I was just - "

"C'mon. I've got something to show you."

I sighed, and followed her out of the shop. She led the way through the precinct until we were standing on a draughty corner near a sad strand of a tree which someone official had planted to commemorate something - but the plaque was smashed and nobody could remember what it was.

Debi's hands were plunged deep inside the pockets of her blue jacket. The early autumn wind whipped my hair as I watched her pull out a small bag. She took the contents out. It was a brand new CD of Debi's favourite band, Noxide.

"Wow! That must've cost you a bit. I thought you said you didn't have much money."

"Don't be daft, Sammy! I didn't pay for it!"
"Eh?"
"Don't be so stupid! You know that boy who works in 'Sounds'? He used to go out with my sister. He let me have it. Free."

"You mean he bought it for you?"

"Sammy! Are you being deliberately stupid?"

My jaw fell open. Debi had stolen the CD. The boy had helped her. I was shocked. I'd always thought Debi was a bit dim but I never imagined she was a thief!

"Oh, Sammy, you should just see your face! Tell you what, we'll go back later, if you like, and get you a CD by The View...that new one you were looking at. OK?" She frowned and rubbed her hands together. "I wish I had some gloves. My hands are cold. Let's go to Fay's Fashions."

I was suddenly terribly afraid that a police officer might jump out of the crowd and arrest us both.

"Debi - the CD - Debi! You can't do this!"

She started giggling. "Don't be silly. I do it every Saturday. Oh, you're not going to go all stuffy and boring about this, are you? Look, we'll go to Fay's Fashions. All right?"

I grabbed her arm. No way was I going to Fay's Fashions with her! I didn't dare! There was no telling what Debi might do in a clothes shop! I wished I was with Amanda. She might be a dreary shopper, but she certainly never shoplifted anything!

"What's up, Sammy? Wouldn't you like something nice and new to wear when you see your boy? Sammy? Are you all right?"

"Debi, you can't - oh!"

I'd just seen 'my boy'.

Luce was standing in the doorway of a jeweller's shop nearby. He looked great; he was wearing blue jeans and a black sweatshirt. He kept checking his watch, his fair hair flopping across his forehead, the dark roots showing ever so slightly. Instantly I forgot everything but him!

"Luce!"

He looked up, and his face broke into that wonderful smile.

"Hey! Samantha!"

And then - and then - a really pretty girl of about eighteen with long dark brown hair came out of the jeweller's. She wasn't wearing very much, even though it was quite a chilly day; just a black crop top and a short white skirt.

"Did you get it?" asked Luce.

"Yeah." She showed him a bracelet she was wearing. "Antony Lucas, I do love you!" And she slung her arms round his neck - and kissed him!

"See you later, Samantha!" Luce put an arm round the girl. She looked at me because he'd spoken to me, and a knowing smile crept onto her wide, crimson mouth. As they walked off together I heard her laugh and say, "Another member of your ever-growing fan club?"

I had never felt such complete devastation in the whole of my life. No, not ever.

Debi was rattling away but all I cared about was Luce with his arm round that girl, and them both staring into each other's eyes as if they were madly in love, and that girl laughing and saying I was a member of his fan club! Oh! How that hurt! With a pang of guilt, I remembered Debi saying exactly the same thing about Dinah just a little while ago! How awful it was being on the receiving end of that taunt. I couldn't bear it. I bit my lip to stop the tears.

"Sammy? Did you hear me? I said, 'I do like Amanda, but I think she's a bit of a show off sometimes, don't you? Especially about her looks?'"

I glanced at Debi Daley and felt sick. "I'm going home. I don't feel too good."

"Sammy, you know, you do look ill, come to mention it. Maybe you've caught that cold you said your mum's got. Yes, you'd better go home. I don't want to catch a horrid bug."

I didn't say goodbye to her. I turned my back and pushed through crowds of Saturday shoppers. On the bus, people were chattering, laughing and talking, their ordinary lives unshaken by any of the horrible events that had happened in mine.

My world seemed to be crashing around my ears. I felt lost and crushed. My romantic fantasy about Luce was over - he didn't really like me at all, he had a girlfriend! A beautiful girlfriend, confident, older than me, someone who looked much more gorgeous than I ever would! Why had I been so stupid as to imagine Luce would ever want to spend any time at all with me, when he could get any beauty he wanted? There'd be no marvellous dates and boasting about it at school! No; in fact there probably wouldn't be any school at all, at least not this one! After all, when Mum couldn't pay the bills we'd have to go and live with my aunt and I'd have to go to Kendra's school!

"Oh God!" I rested my head against the window as the bus rumbled on, "Oh God, help me!"

I realised what I was saying, and groaned.

Why would God want to listen to me, now that I had trouble? I'd shoved him away, hadn't I, more or less told him not to bother me, even though I'd felt the awesome reality of his Presence when I'd encountered him on Thursday! I groaned again. Yes, he'd been trying to speak to me, hadn't he, but I'd tried to shut him out because I didn't want him inconveniently challenging my new 'cool' status!

I'd wanted to be grown-up, but look how I'd behaved lately! Was it really adult behaviour? I'd turned into quite an accomplished liar; I'd lied to my mum, and been downright horrible to caring Bob and poor little Dinah. And what had I been doing that afternoon? Hanging around with a girl who stole - *stole* - a CD from 'Sounds', quite blatantly, shamelessly, and didn't seem at all bothered about what she'd done! Thoughts whirled round my brain. Perhaps I should've made her return the CD - I didn't know; I hadn't thought about it once I'd seen Luce!

I didn't feel cool and grown-up at all. I felt small and mean and bad.

I wiped my tears away with the back of my hand as I got off the bus.

I'd pushed God away. Now that I wanted to ask him for help, I just couldn't!

Could I?

But if he wouldn't help, who would?

By The River

"Just because I can't go to church this morning, there's no reason why you shouldn't go."

I was tempted to tell yet another lie and say I thought I'd caught Mum's cold and didn't feel well enough to go to church, but I saw Mrs Kettle bustling up the drive and decided I'd go out after all.

It was a cloudy morning. There were a few puddles in the gutter, and the grey sky promised more rain. I turned the collar up on my jacket. I was glad it was a miserable day, because I felt miserable.

As I scuffed along, I spotted some people I knew, heading for the church. They were chattering together, apparently excited at the prospect of going to worship Jesus that morning. They seemed so full of life, and I felt so low I didn't want to be anywhere near them. So I turned away before they could see me, and dawdled along a long straight road called South Street.

I didn't really know where I was going that morning or what I was going to do. I sauntered aimlessly down the street. Most of the shops were shut and there was a peculiar Sunday morning feeling that was difficult to define. Ahead, I could see the leaves of a horse chestnut tree by the bridge were beginning to turn orange and yellow. I thought, I'll go and sit by the river for a while. Maybe Mum won't find out I wasn't at church.

The little river that flowed through Millstead was actually less like a river than a large stream.

I walked along a grassy path wedged between it and the start of a trading estate and slumped down on an iron bench. Across the water stood several new, expensive looking houses, as yet unlived in, an old cottage, and a jetty with a row-boat. A man was in the cottage garden, with a machine that looked like a vacuum, sucking up the few leaves that had dared to stray onto his lawn. I thought he must live a very pointless and boring life if that was all he had to do on a Sunday morning. But then, maybe he was thinking the same sort of thing about me.

For a while, I didn't think about anything much, just how horrid life was. I seemed to see Luce and that girl kissing like a video playing in my mind. Then I remembered Kendra telling me "You silly kid. As if a boy like that would ever give you a second glance!" and Mum saying, "Plays with dolls!" and tried to imagine what it would be like living in the same house as Kendra and Aunty Ann and going to a brand new school where all Kendra's probably horrible friends went.

"Oh, God!"

It had started to rain ever so slightly. Raindrops danced on the water.

"Oh, God! God!"

Whether or not he heard me or didn't want to be bothered with me anymore, just as I hadn't wanted to be bothered with him, I suddenly felt an urgent and overwhelming need to find him. What had Bob said at the youth club that time? 'Seek and you will find'...

"Oh, everything is just so terrible! Oh God! Where are you? Where are you?"

Something popped into my brain. Mum had

said Jesus was the Door. And Bob's voice seemed to echo in my mind, too. Jesus was the Gate. I knew that if I wanted to get in touch with God, right then, it had to start with Jesus.

All right, I thought.

"Jesus!" I took a deep breath. "Jesus! Jesus! JESUS!"

And as I called on that Name, something happened.

He was there.

Yes, he was, and I was immediately aware of it. How? It was the reality of his Presence - which I had first felt in our kitchen when I was looking in the fridge. And a Presence I realised I'd first perceived when I was very small. I felt my heart lift. He hadn't said, "Oh well, you don't want to know me, goodbye!" after all. He was right here with me, in the rain, by the river, and I knew it.

"Oh Jesus!" Tears trickled down my face. I felt I was in the presence of a real Friend who loved me. The words came flooding out, now. "Oh Jesus, please help me, my life is such a mess! I wanted to be grown-up, Lord! But it's all horrible!" And I realised that he knew exactly how horrible everything was. He knew all about me and my life. And he cared.

I immediately knew something else, too.

I had a choice. I was at a crossroads, just like Bob had said. I had to either ask Jesus into my life properly, or turn my back on him. I couldn't have it both ways. Jesus wanted me to follow him wholeheartedly.

But I'd wanted a new life. A changed life. A grown-up life. Following Jesus wouldn't make me popular with my friends. I'd be even more of a God Botherer in their eyes than before! I bit my lip and searched in my pocket for some gum, but I'd left it at home.

"Oh Lord, if I do ask you into my life, I think I can say goodbye to being Cool!"

He was waiting. I could sense it.

Thousands of consequences for my actions in the next minute jumped about in my mind. But one thing shone out amongst them. I didn't want to lose that wonderful Presence, that feeling of love and warmth and security that came from Jesus - the confident feeling that I wouldn't be alone anymore, but that I could have a real Friend who would always be with me, no matter what.

"Jesus! Come into my life. I can't deny what I know to be real. You want me to give my whole life to you - I will, Lord. I will! Oh Lord, I think it's going to be very hard. Please help me!"

He'd been trying to reveal himself to me for some time now. I remembered with startling clarity things Bob and mum had said that had really hit me with force. I realised it was Jesus himself, using their words to call me to come to him. I sat there, quite overawed for a minute that he should care so much for me. But there was something I had to do before I went any further.

"Lord, I'm so sorry for all the things I've said and done to hurt you and other people - I was awful to Dinah, and really terrible to Bob. And I've lied to Mum - and I've made friends with someone who doesn't like you at all and who steals things! Lord! I tried to go to a pub!" Other things came to mind as I spoke, and I rattled them out, wanting to be completely right with Jesus from the outset. Then I felt a wonderful wave of love and peace washing over me, and felt completely forgiven and accepted by him. It was marvellous.

Incredibly, I felt like a new person - not like the dreary girl who'd plonked herself down on that seat just fifteen minutes before. Jesus had come to live in my heart by his Spirit, and he was going to help me be a real Christian and live for him. And I started laughing.

"Oh Lord!" I said, "You're the one who can give us really new changed lives! How stupid I was to think clothes or make-up could make me different! It's to do with something on the inside, isn't it, not the outside, and only you can do it!"

Yes, that new life I'd been hoping to get had turned up in the shape of Jesus, the minute I'd laid my own pathetic efforts down. It wasn't the changed and different life I'd been striving for - I had a feeling it was going to be far better.

I felt like dancing.

The man who was sucking up the leaves had no idea that such a momentous change had happened whilst he was so engrossed in his work. But he heard me shouting "Wow!" and glanced up, and I waved to him.

He didn't wave back.

"Oh wow!"

Jesus was a real and living person, not just a figure in a book or someone the minister spoke about on Sundays, someone other people knew and I didn't!

"He's my Friend! I'm going to follow him and

he's going to help me!"

I nearly exploded with excitement. And it occurred to me that you could go to church week after week and pray and do loads of things for God and never ever really meet him! It was an incredible thought. After all, everyone - including me - had thought I was a Christian, hadn't they, just because I went to church youth club and C.U. and knew a bit about the Bible? But I'd never asked Jesus into my heart as my personal Saviour before.

It was raining quite hard now. I felt the moment had come for me to go home. I almost ran, feeling I could just about fly with joy.

Mrs Kettle had gone, and Mum was moving slowly about the kitchen. I felt a sudden powerful surge of love towards her. I suddenly saw that most of her over-protective ways stemmed from the fact that she'd had to bring me up alone without a dad being there. And I thought, she may not be perfect but she does love Jesus. And wow, does she love me!

"You're wet!" she observed, crossly.

"Don't worry, Mum!" I put my arm round her shoulders.

"How come you're so wet? Didn't you take an umbrella? If you catch a cold - "

"I'm fine. Best ever. And it'll all be OK. We've got Jesus, haven't we? He'll sort it all out."

She looked at me, stunned, and I wondered if she thought I was being facetious. She kept watching me, sideways, as I made some hot buttered toast and I suppose she must've wondered what sort of church service I'd been to that had transformed the dismal girl of that morning into somebody who was almost as bouncy as Bob. But she didn't ask. She went back to bed for the afternoon and said she didn't want to be disturbed for a bit. I got the impression she wanted to pray.

I had a feeling I was going to be included in those prayers.

I don't know what Mum thought when I went into her room at six o'clock and smilingly said I was going to church. I didn't make any excuses not to go and wasn't at all reluctant, and I think she was about to ask me if I felt quite well but she had a huge coughing fit and couldn't. For the first time in ever so long, I actually wanted to go. I really wanted to see Bob and tell him what had happened to me - I wondered how I could ever have thought him childish; he really knew Jesus, didn't he, and God had really used Bob in my coming to know him.

It was still raining, and there weren't many people at the evening service; just the minister and a handful of old people. I was disappointed to see that Bob wasn't there.

We sang a few old hymns, the sort that normally made me yawn and my eyes wander around the dreary whitewashed walls. But this evening things were different. The hymns and songs I'd sung for years seemed to really mean something at last. The words were real. They leapt out of the song book at me. Then the minister stood up and said there were quite a few folk from the church who were sick. He mentioned my mum and Mr Upson, and I remembered that God had told ancient Mr Upson to pray for me. Only God could really have known what was happening in my life; he knew about all that turmoil. I'd always just thought of Mr Upson as a sad old man, but my opinion of him changed that evening as I realised he must really be in tune with Jesus. I decided to return the compliment and pray for him too, so I screwed my eyes up tightly and silently asked God to sort out Mr Upson and make him full of health.

"That was great!" I beamed at the minister, as we filed out of the church.

The minister - a bald man called Mr Skinner who was actually a postman when he wasn't ministering - looked down at his hand which was red because I was pumping it so vigorously and gave me the sort of sideways glance my mum had, earlier.

I was bursting. I just had to tell someone.

"I've asked Jesus into my heart. Really asked him. I feel different!"

Now the minister's face broke into a wide smile and he was pumping *my* hand.

"Well, isn't that something! Praise God!"

"I've been coming to church for ages. But I never knew him before. Not really and truly. Can you believe it?"

Mr Skinner nodded, wisely. "Yes, Samantha. Well! This is marvellous. Praise the Lord!"

"Er - perhaps we ought to stop shaking hands. People are staring."

"What? Oh yes. Samantha, you've told me some wonderful news tonight. Very encouraging."

I guessed he needed encouraging; our church was going through a strange time just then, with half the people wanting the old-fashioned kind of service we'd had tonight, and half wanting to start raising their hands in worship and play guitars, and both halves feeling cross about the other half.

"Bless you, Samantha!" he said.

I walked away from the church feeling I could float on air. I wished Bob had been there; I wished Dinah had, too, but she didn't come to our church, just the youth club - which had a great reputation far and wide. I thought she went to a church across town but I didn't know which one.

"I really ought to tell Mum, too," I said to myself. So I did, as soon as I got home. At first she was shocked because she thought I'd given my life to the Lord years ago. Then she looked thrilled and hugged me and I felt even more happy.

I went on feeling that way even when I woke up the next morning, and as I walked to school, I felt excited at the prospect of seeing Dinah and Mrs Foster and telling them what had happened to me - although I also knew I had to apologise to Dinah for being so nasty to her on Saturday.

Then, as I walked, something odd happened - a malevolent voice whispered in my ear.

"Your new popularity is going to take a nosedive if you share your story at school!"

"I know. It's all right. I don't care! I'm following Jesus!"

But the insidious thought wouldn't leave me.

"Look, there's the school gates. It's OK thinking you don't care about not being cool anymore when you're on your own, but what about when you're with Amanda and Debi and the rest ? Imagine their faces if you say you've met Jesus and he's real and you're going to follow him. They'll never understand it! They'll just think Sammy's being religious and churchy and boring again."

My heart was sinking.

"You know what you can do?" said the voice. "You can keep it quiet. You'll still be a Christian but no-one need ever know! You can be a secret Christian! Maybe that way you can even keep some of your new 'cool' after all!"

"Oh, yes!" I nodded to myself. "Great idea!" I bit my lip. What about C.U.? I really wanted to start going to C.U. again. What would my friends say to that? I sighed; I'd have to be really, really smart and think of something...maybe it wouldn't hurt if I just didn't go to C.U...kept my Christian activities to out of school time...

The wind seemed chillier than before as I turned in through the school gates. And did I imagine it, or was the Lord's presence not so warm and real to me anymore?

I put some gum in my mouth and frowned. Jesus wanted me to follow him whole-heartedly. Didn't he!

"But I am! I will! I'm just going to be sort of quiet about it at school, that's all!"

"Hey, Sammy!"

Some of the girls in my class were standing nearby.

"Sammy! How was your weekend?"

"Did you see your boyfriend? Where did you go? Anywhere nice?"

My boyfriend! I thought of Luce. Kissing that girl.

"Hi," I said, as coolly as I could, "Anyone seen Amanda?"

"In the cloakrooms, probably."

"Thanks!"

I swiftly marched off, congratulating myself on dodging their questions. I felt confident, now; the issue of my faith would never come up, if I was careful. And I was sure God wouldn't mind. Would he?

I've learned since that sometimes, we may decide things, but God has different ideas. I was blissfully unaware as I walked to the cloakrooms, that I was about to discover this was one of those times.

Taking Sides

I walked right into the middle of it.

The cloakrooms were unusually empty, except for a small knot of girls in one corner that I didn't take much notice of at first.

But then, I was just about to go and wash my hands, when I heard a frightened squeal that made me stop and glance over at the girls. One was Trina Finch.

"This is her, Trina! I call her the Saint. She makes me sick with all that Bible-bashing rubbish! She thinks she's better than us!"

"No, I don't!"

Another squeal.

"Yes you do, and my sister's going to teach you a lesson! I told you she would!"

"Jesus!"

"Don't think he's gonna help you! No-one is!"

For a moment I couldn't believe what I was witnessing.

"Dinah!"

She was backing up, and then bumping into a row of wash-basins. Her face was a picture of sheer terror. I recognised one of the other girls now as Trina's younger sister, and there were two others that I didn't know.

"Ha, ha, Saint Dinah!" sneered Trina Finch's sister, "Start praying, Saint! My sister's going to kill you for what you said about our mum!"

"Yeah, what is all this?" Trina leaned towards Dinah in a very menacing fashion. "Tanya says you called our mum a witch because she makes corn dollies for harvest festival!"

"I didn't!" Dinah cried, "I said - "

"Who cares what you said!" growled one of the other kids.

"I do!" said Trina, "I don't like to hear someone's been telling lies about my family!"

"Let's flush her head down the loo!" said Trina's sister, with a very malicious grin.

"Jesus! Help me!" shrieked Dinah.

Trina glared at her. "Let's get to the bottom of this!"

The other girls made a lunge for Dinah and tried to pin her arms behind her back.

"Oi!" I said, without thinking, "Stop that, right now!"

Trina Finch glared round. She really did look like a boy in a dress. I found myself sending up a quick prayer - "Jesus!"

"Sammy. Stay out of it. OK?"

"Sammy! Sammy! Thank God you're here! Help!" cried Dinah.

"Shut up!" said Trina, roughly.

I wasn't sure what Trina honestly expected to do to Dinah, whether she was really going to stick her head down the loo, or if I could stop her if she tried. I doubted it. She could make mincemeat out of me if she wanted to. But I couldn't leave Dinah to her mercy, could I!

"Jesus! Help!" I prayed again.

"What's going on?"

I had never been so relieved in my life as I was right then when I heard Debi Daley's voice.

She - and Amanda - had walked in behind me, with some other girls from our year. Their entrance couldn't have been better timed and I thanked God silently and profusely.

"Trina Finch!" sniffed Debi, "Beating up little children? Shame on you!"

"This brat insulted my mum!" Trina's rather brutal features were fixed into an aggressive mask. "She's not getting away with it."

"Oh really!" Debi went to one of the washbasins and ran the water. "You bully, Trina!"

"Shut up, airhead!" snapped Trina, "It's none of your business!"

The younger kids I didn't know seemed a bit nervous now they could see some older people were involved. But Trina's sister, Tanya, still had a spiteful look on her face and seemed angry when Dinah escaped from the fumbling clutches of her friends and ran to the rest of us.

"Let it go, Trina," I said, "She's only a kid."

"She said our mum was a witch," replied Tanya, vindictively.

"I didn't say that!" Dinah was obviously feeling more brave now that we were there, "You said your mum made corn dollies and I said I didn't like them because they were something to do with a pagan goddess and I was a Christian and believed in Jesus."

"She's at it again!" Tanya fumed, "She's always talking about Jesus! It drives me mad!"

"I love him, why shouldn't I talk about him?" said Dinah, stubbornly, "He's alive!"

Amanda looked at Dinah. "Why don't you just say sorry for - well, whatever - then Trina and the others will let you alone. OK?"

"All right, kid," said Trina, glancing at the rest of us, her fury apparently subsiding, and seeming a bit embarrassed now at being caught intimidating a youngster, "You've upset my sister and you've insulted my mum. But pack it in and say sorry, right now, and we'll let it drop. All right?"

"Let it drop? We ought to flush her head - " began Tanya, but Trina told her to shut up and she did.

"I'm sorry you don't like what I said," Dinah told Trina's sister.

"That's not an apology!" said Trina.

"But I'm right." Dinah looked at me, confidently. "Aren't I, Sammy? Jesus is alive!"

There were an awful lot of girls crowding into the cloakroom, and they all heard what was being said.

"Sammy?" said Dinah, "Sammy, tell them!"

Every eye was on me; Debi was glancing over her shoulder, with a half-mocking smile on her face. Amanda was frowning at me, quizzically. Trina looked exasperated and her sister, resentful. The rest were just looking. At me.

It seemed to me to get very hot just then.

I groaned, inwardly. I'd been hoping to keep my beliefs a secret, hadn't I?

Now what?

If I said "Look, kid, don't be so silly, just apologise and shut up!" I'd probably get nods of approval but I'd deny something I knew without doubt was true.

But if I said anything else I was likely not only to be totally Uncool for ever more but also maybe get my head flushed down the same pan as Dinah either now - or in the future.

It was a frightening thought.

I swallowed hard.

"Oh, Jesus!"

It was all very well saying I knew Jesus but it was no use at all if I didn't really believe in him. And if I really did I had to stand up for him. Right then I saw that you couldn't really be a secret believer at all. You were either for Jesus, or not. I took a deep breath. What had Bob said? The narrow road of following Jesus wasn't easy at all? He wasn't kidding.

I had to take sides. It was important. I had to do it right now.

"Yes, Dinah. Jesus is alive."

Even as I said it, I felt somehow stronger than I ever had and all the fear I'd felt drained away. I knew Jesus was with me. I smiled, because I knew Jesus had allowed this to happen. I guessed it was maybe the first test of my faith. I thought, I passed! Whatever happens next, I passed! I didn't feel scared at all now as I faced the others. I felt very calm.

Debi rolled her eyes. Trina clenched her fists. Tanya cursed. Then the bell for registration went.

"Thank you Lord!" I said, under my breath.

"Sammy Jones!" Trina looked as me with a half sneer, "God Botherer! Did anyone ever think you were cool? I don't think so!"

She stalked out of the cloakrooms.

"And don't think I've finished with you!" Tanya craftily punched Dinah in the side on the way out.

"Yes you have," I called after her, "And you better believe it."

"Ouch!" Dinah rubbed her side. "Sammy! You coming just then was an answer to prayer. It was, Sammy. They'd have murdered me. I'd have been a martyr!"

"I don't think it would have been quite as bad as that! Still, bad enough. Are you OK?"

"Yes. Jesus rescued me, Sammy. He sent help."

"Yes. He rescued you. I think he rescued both of us."

"Sammy, I was trying to tell you on Saturday that I'd been threatened!"

"Hmm. Dinah, I'm sorry I didn't listen to you. I was horrible."

Dinah looked shy. "It's OK."

"I've got things to tell you, Dinah. Something's happened to me."

The others all left the cloakroom, murmuring in quiet voices, the drama already replaced in their minds by important issues such as an impending history test and a geography project deadline and netball and who was going out with whom. I rested my forehead against one of the mirrors above the basins.

"D'you know, I quite admire that," said Amanda, quietly.

"What?"

"I dunno. Just that you really stuck up for what you believe. I don't think I could've done that. That's brave. And pretty cool, you know."

I looked at her in surprise. She offered me a stick of chewing gum. And I knew that it wasn't really me who was brave and cool. Dinah was. Why had I ever called her Drippy Dinah? She was Daring Dinah! She spoke up for Jesus and wasn't worried what others thought about that; even when she knew she might be horribly bullied. And I felt suddenly ashamed. I'd behaved so badly to Dinah, and yet I could see that she really was brimming with faith in Jesus. She'd always admired me - but I knew now I had a lot to learn from her.

"You weren't quite you without the religious bit," said Amanda.

"Amanda, I - "

Before I could continue, Debi spoke. "Tragic. I think it's tragic!"

"What is?" asked Amanda.

Debi was peering in one of the mirrors. "Look. A big red spot on my nose. Oh my goodness. No-one will fancy me anymore. This is a tragedy. What am I going to do?"

I shook my head. How could I ever have thought it good to be equal with poor, sad Debi! What a twit I'd been.

"You might start," I said, "By taking that CD back to 'Sounds'."

Debi looked shocked. Then she began giggling because she thought I was joking. Then she remembered her spot and started complaining again, before locking herself in a cubicle, still moaning.

Amanda tapped me on the shoulder. "Do you want to come round tonight?"

"Aren't you seeing Tank?"

She shrugged. "I dunno. He's quite boring, really. All he talks about is football."

114

I felt a little tug at my sleeve.

"I've got to go to my class, now, Sammy. But I was wondering. Would you like to come to tea at my house sometime?"

I could just imagine Debi making a sarcastic remark about hanging out with little kids but I didn't care about that anymore. "Yes, Dinah. Thanks. I'd love that."

Amanda and I walked out of the cloakrooms.

"Oh dear," she said, "We've forgotten Debi."

"Oops."

Amanda hesitated momentarily and then flicked her hair back. "Do we have to keep hanging around with her? I know you've become quite friendly lately, but I'm getting a bit fed up with her, aren't you?"

I smiled at her. "Right. Definitely."

At Amanda's house later on, I did try to explain to her exactly what had happened to me on Sunday. I don't really know if she understood a word of what I was saying, because she looked quite blank and said she'd always thought I was a Christian anyway because I went to church and stuff. I tried to tell her that you could go to church all your life and never really be a Christian because you didn't have a personal relationship with God through his Son Jesus. I also said that I was going to be different from now on because I had Jesus in my heart by his Spirit and she said she thought I'd already said I was going to change anyway.

At that point I gave up and we talked about the boys in The View instead. Then I told Amanda about Luce and the girl and she sympathised and said never mind, perhaps it wasn't serious and he might finish with her. And I felt a sudden hope.

Amanda's mother drove me home. The streets flashed past to an accompaniment of 1970s pop music and idle chat as I decided I was going to pray and pray and pray for Amanda to come to know Jesus. Perhaps I'd also pray for Luce - pray that he'd finish with his girl! I could even pray he'd ask me out! I grinned as I thought about that.

But God had ideas about the Luce situation, and he was about to make them very apparent.

It was nine o'clock when I slammed the car door and waved goodbye to Amanda's mum. The evening was quite cold. I started to think a few months ahead to Christmas, wondering whether it would be any different now that I really knew Jesus. I had a feeling it was going to be a lot more special than ever before.

I was ambling up the path when the van belonging to Des, the lodger, drew up. I glanced round as two men got out. The one who'd been in the passenger seat seemed to be having a difficult time walking and clutched at the van's bonnet in an apparent effort to steady himself.

"Luce!"

Yes, it was Luce - but not like I'd ever seen him. He didn't seem able to get his balance. He was giggling crazily, but Des wasn't. Luce stumbled and I gasped. He looked so different; not handsome and gorgeous at all - rough and haggard and gaunt with his hair sticking up.

"Come on, mate," said Des. He saw me as he put an arm round Luce. "Oh, hello, love. Don't look so worried; he's OK. Sort of. The idiot - he's been at The Black Dog all day."

I didn't understand what he meant - till I realised that Luce was horrendously drunk.

I watched as Des helped Luce to their front door. I'd never seen anyone drunk before. It was awful. Especially when Luce stopped giggling, lurched forward and threw up on the door step.

"Oh, yuk!"

Des dragged Luce indoors.

"Yuk!"

I never ever fancied him again after that. And all I could think was how horrid it had been to see him out of control and drunk and I wondered how I could ever have wanted to be his girl - and why I ever thought pubs were 'grown-up' places to be.

A Different Life

"You're really growing up. I'm proud of you."

I must've looked stunned, because Mum started laughing.

"What's wrong? You should see your face."

"Eh? Oh - nothing. I just wondered what made you say that, Mum."

Mum leaned back on her swivelly office chair and smiled.

"Well, what did you just say to me?"

"I said I thought I might visit Mr Upson this weekend. Take some chocolates or something."

"There you are."

"So that means I'm growing up?"

I shook my head. I'd never understand adults in a zillion years.

"Are you going to take a break soon, Mum?"

"Hmm? Oh yes - soon."

She'd told me that all day long she'd been phoning and writing letters. I looked down at her concerned face. She'd coped for so long on her own to bring me up and pay our bills and everything. Only she hadn't really been alone, had she? Jesus was with her.

"Mum, I do love you. I'd never swap you."

"Oh - good - I'm pleased to hear it!"

"Mum, do you think you'll get more clients?"

"I hope so. But I don't know; I still think the answer may have to be a move."

I could hardly bring myself to utter the words, but I did. "To Aunty Ann's?"

"Well, yes, at first." Mum bit the end of her pen. "It seems to be an ideal solution."

Ideal wasn't a word I'd have used about it, but I knew I couldn't start moaning and being selfish and giving Mum more stress saying I didn't want to move.

"I'd better go, Mum." I put my jacket on and wondered where I'd left my latest packet of chewing gum.

"Don't forget to ask Bob to give you a lift home!"

I turned to her, the well-known feeling of irritation creeping up on me.

"I thought you said I was growing up?"

"Well, you are, but there are still a lot of weird people about. Especially at night. You've got to be careful, Sam."

"But - " I stopped. Her face was full of motherly anxiety. I swallowed down my irritation. After all, she just loved me, didn't she? I bent down and kissed her. "All right, Mum. I'll be careful."

I went downstairs, and as I set off for the youth club meeting, I saw Mrs Kettle trotting across the road towards our house and thought that Mum wouldn't be at all pleased to have a visitor when she was so busy.

I felt a sudden compassion for Mrs Kettle. I'd never felt it before, so it occurred to me that it must be something from God. But it struck me that she might be a bit lonely. I'd never thought about that. Maybe I ought to add Mrs Kettle to the list of people to pray for. It was getting quite long; there were the Christians I knew, and Amanda, and even Debi. Also, although

119

I really didn't want to, I knew I should pray for people I didn't like much, as well - people like Trina Finch and her sister. And, of course, I ought to pray for Kendra and Dorian and Aunty Ann, too. They all needed Jesus. After all, my aunt was continually looking to all sorts of alternative spiritual things that didn't meet her deep needs. I knew that only Jesus could give her real peace and security and love inside.

I was a bit late for the youth club meeting. They were already jumping around playing some idiotic game. As soon as I pushed open the door and saw them, a wave of depression crept over me. I'd hoped I'd feel more positive about joining in with the group of kids again now I was a real Christian. But I didn't.

"Oh Jesus! I'd really like to meet Christians my own age!"

The kids had spotted me, so I tried to appear cheerful.

"Sammy!" yelled Dinah.

"Hey!" called Bob.

I sat down on the stage. Bob came over and sat down beside me as the kids started playing another game. He looked even more like a golden retriever than usual, all excited and out of breath.

"Hey, Sammy. It's good to see you!"

"Bob! Before you say anything, I'm sorry I spoke to you like I did the other day."

"Eh? Oh - that's all right. At least you were honest."

"Bob, I've got something to tell you." Even as I prepared to tell him my good news, the rather squashed feelings I'd been experiencing went away. I grinned a broad grin. "I've met Jesus. I asked him into my heart just as you said I should."

He smiled.

"You know!" I cried, "How do you know?"

"What, Sammy, do you think the minister never talks to me?"

We both burst out laughing.

"It's great, Sammy. Great."

He gave me a great big bear hug, and I got a face full of his woolly jumper. When I managed to extricate myself, I said, "I tried to phone you to tell you, but you've been out!" in between picking bits of wool out of my mouth.

"Yes, I've been very busy meeting with other youth leaders this week." Bob took a large white handkerchief out of his jeans pocket and mopped his brow with it. "Actually, I've got something to talk to you about. But first of all, do you fancy sharing your testimony with the others? It would be fantastic for the kids to hear this, I'm sure."

My testimony!

I had a testimony!

I was quite thrilled at the thought.

Bob called the kids over, and said Sammy had something to tell them. They all sat down on the floor. And I told them all about how I met Jesus. Afterwards, Dinah said it was like something out of the book Mrs Foster had been reading to them at C.U.

"It's called ' True Stories, Changed Lives'," said Dinah.

"That's what I've got, Dinah. A true story and a changed life. I feel different inside. I think it's what the Bible calls being born again. It's like a whole new Sammy, right and clean before God, has sort of

121

replaced the old one."

Then, Bob gave a little talk about how much Jesus loved people, so much that he came to give them peace with God and a new life to be lived in his power because we couldn't live good lives without his help. After that the kids squirmed about, and someone asked if they could play another game. And they all begged me to join in, so I reluctantly prepared to do so.

"Sammy!" Bob turned to me just as I was going to arrange some chairs for the game. "Before we start - I was talking to the youth leader at the Parkside Christian Fellowship. You know - that big new church in the middle of town? They have a huge youth group with loads of teenagers every Friday night. I just wondered if you'd like to give that a try? I mean, it'd be nice if you made some Christian friends of your own age and older, wouldn't it?"

For a minute, I was stunned and couldn't quite register what he was saying. Then I did and my jaw dropped open rather unattractively.

"I just prayed about that as I came in!"

"Well, there you are! God's amazing, isn't he!"

"Wow! Unreal!"

"I can arrange for someone to give you a lift there," said Bob, "If you're interested. Which I take it you are!"

"Am I ever!"

Dinah was nearby and heard what we were saying.

"Oh, Sammy, my brother goes to that youth club - Tim, who's at the grammar school," commented Dinah, "Oh! I'd forgotten to tell you, Sammy. My brother's coming to - "

One of the other kids interrupted. "Sammy, you'll still come to this club as well won't you?"

Then it hit me. I might not be living in Millstead for much longer so I very likely wouldn't be coming to this youth club or going to the interesting new one. I felt my joy at the prospect of meeting Christians my own age drain away.

"What's up?" said Bob, "Not worried your mum's going to say no? I'm sure she won't. I bet she'll be excited that you're going to such a lively church youth group. They do all sorts of interesting things - help out with street evangelism, go on camps, see live bands - "

The more he spoke about the wonderful new group, the more low I felt. In the end, I felt I had to shut him up or I'd burst into tears of frustration. So I clapped my hands together, smiled brightly and said, "C'mon, kids! Let's have a really riotous game, shall we?"

I entered into the spirit of the game with all my might just to forget my troubles. I also managed to forget how I looked or how old I was and everything else as I began to have real fun. In the end, we all fell in a heap on the floor, exhausted and giggling. It was then that I realised a really good looking boy of about fifteen had appeared and was standing by the stage, watching.

"Tim!" shouted Dinah, "Tim, this is Sammy."

The boy walked over and looked at me. And I realised I must look a complete fright, all hot and messy and scruffy.

"Sammy," said Dinah, breathlessly, "this is my brother."

He grinned at me. "I had to come and see this girl who rescued my sister and stood up for Jesus!"

"What? Oh! Well, I didn't really rescue her. I mean, it wasn't just me. I mean - "

I stopped speaking as my hair fell across my face. I pushed it away. Dinah's brother was gazing at me with kind hazel eyes. I had a feeling that this boy was more interested in who I was rather than what I looked like.

"I think it was a cool thing to do, standing up for your faith like that," he said.

"Like what?" asked Bob.

"Coo-eee!"

Everyone looked at the door.

"Oh no!"

It was my mum.

Yes, it was, she was standing there, with a dripping umbrella making puddles on the floor. I almost died of embarrassment. My mum had come to meet me from youth club - just when I'd met a new boy!

"Hello, Mrs Jones!" cried Bob, "Come in. Everyone, you all know Sammy's mum!"

"I'm sorry to interrupt," she said, coming over, and I could see her face was all red and shiny with happiness. "But I've got such wonderful news I couldn't keep it to myself until Samantha came home. Sam! You won't believe what's happened!"

I stood up. "Mum! Is it something to do with your work? Have Fothergill's given you your job back?"

"No. It's Mrs Kettle." Mum laughed as she saw my perplexed look. "She's got this friend from her amateur dramatics society - he's something to do with that big builders' merchants in South Street. He wants someone to do his accounts! And guess what, she's told him all about me, and he's just been to see me, and I've got a job! A good one! A proper job, nine to five!"

"Oh! Mum!"

"Isn't it wonderful? What an answer to prayer!"

I grasped her arm in excitement.

"Does that mean we won't be going to live with Aunty Ann after all?"

"What? Of course it does. That was only an idea."

"Oh, wow! Yes! Great! Oh! Thank you Jesus! Thank you, thank you!"

Later, I climbed into Bob's car as he locked the church hall. Mum was in the front seat, animated and full of happy chatter. I looked at the street lights and red car tail lights reflected through the drops of rain on the car windows, feeling quite overcome by events.

"This is incredible," I thought, "I just asked Jesus into my life and he's doing so much already I can hardly catch my breath. He knows all my needs - he knows what's best. He really does. Wow. I'm going to trust him with everything forever."

As Bob got in the car and we set off on our journey home, I couldn't help but wonder at the awesomeness of God. I'd so much wanted to have a changed life. I'd gone about it all in the wrong way. But meeting Jesus, I'd got a different life all right - one he'd given me and would help me to live.

We reached our house, and Mum sped to the front door as driving rain beat down, running along the pavements and swirling in the gutters.

Bob smiled at me. "God bless you, Sammy!"

"I'll make mistakes, you know, Bob."

"It's a narrow path. It won't be easy. But it's the true and right path, and he'll be with you, and he'll forgive you when you ask him."

And as I got out of the car and darted home, I knew this was just the start of an adventure with Jesus that was going to last a lifetime. And beyond.

A LITTLE BIT EXTRA

Why not look into these themes from 'A Different Life' and see what you can learn from Sammy's story?

CHANGE
Change is never easy. Whether it's growing up, like Sammy, moving house, losing someone close to you or whatever the change in your life may be, it's good to remember that even when everything else is different, God will always be the same. He never changes.
James 1:17

PEER PRESSURE
It can be especially difficult to be a Christian in school. Sometimes you might feel like just following the crowd, like Sammy did, and keeping quiet about Jesus. Don't! Remember how much Jesus has done for you - he even died for you! So don't ever be ashamed of Jesus and always be ready to speak up for him.
1 Peter 3:15

GETTING ADVICE
Sammy got a bit fed-up with people telling her what she should do. Sometimes you might feel that you're getting advice from all directions - parents, teachers, youth group leaders etc. Don't forget that a lot of their advice will be good advice, given because they care for you and want what's best for you. Above all, remember that God's advice in the Bible can always be trusted. You can totally rely on him!
Isaiah 48:17

RELATIONSHIPS
To begin with, Sammy was mad about Luce. He looked great and she knew her friends would be impressed if he was her boyfriend. But then she found out what he was really like! Remember that God sees what people are like on the inside as well as the outside. Nobody can fool God. So, commit everything about your life to Jesus - you can confidently leave the choice with him.
1 Samuel 16:7

FINDING JESUS
Sammy came to a point where she realised that she needed to find Jesus. You need to see that too. It's not enough for your parents or friends to be Christians - you need to get to know Jesus for yourself. When you do, you'll start living a different life and you won't regret it!
Psalm 34:8
Matthew 6:33

Have you got the other books by the same author?

Sheila Jacobs

Aliens and Strangers

In this book we meet Jane for the very first time. She hates her school and doesn't have many friends. The only thing she enjoys is writing science fiction. But are Jane's stories just fiction? Or have aliens really landed on earth? Is their mission to break up families - will Jane's family be next? Jane discovers there is only one person she can turn to, but will he help her?

ISBN: 1-85792-279-4

Sheila Jacobs

Rollercoaster Time

Jane is desperate to know the future. She is sick fed up of all the ups and downs in her life and she is worried about what lies ahead. Should she try and find out? Someone at school shows Jane a magazine called Future Fantastic that promises to show you the future and what's to come! Astrology! Tarot Cards! Palmistry! Your love life written in the stars. Will Jane be fooled or will she trust the one person who really knows what is round the corner?

ISBN: 1-85792-385-5

Sheila Jacobs

Something to Shout About

Jane is back in her old home town of Gipley but things are not the same as they were, in more ways than one. Heather's mum has got a slimy new boyfriend, Heron introduces everybody to her very good-looking brother, Woody, and it seems as though Heather's church is now going to get closed down. Woody persuades Jane and Heather to spear head a 'Save our Church' campaign. Soon the girls are up to their necks in banners, slogans and campaign strategies. However nobody has thought to ask God what he thinks of the whole situation. Eventually Jane learns a valuable lesson about prayer and seeking God's will in every situation.

ISBN: 1-85792-488-6

Look out for our other

Fiction titles

Twice Freed
by Patricia St. John

Onesimus is a slave in Philemon's household. All he has ever wanted is to live his life in freedom. He wants nothing to do with Jesus Christ or, the man, Paul, who preaches about him.

Onesimus plans to make his escape one day. He gets his chance in the middle of an earthquake. After he manages to steal some money from his master Onesimus sets off for a life of freedom. Along the way he meets friends and enemies and fights for his life as a gladiator in the Roman arena. Will Onesimus escape? Will he one day find his way back to Eireene the beautiful young merchant's daughter? Find out what happens and if Onesimus realises the meaning of true freedom!

ISBN: 185792-489-4

Look out for our other

Fiction titles

Martin's Last Chance
by Heidi Schmidt

Rebekka and Martin live in Germany. They are firm friends and hang out everywhere together. Rebekka has a sweet tooth and a tendency towards shop lifting. Martin is a Christian and wants to introduce Rebekka to the God who loves her - he also wants to stop her from nicking sweets from the corner shop.

Martin, however, has a rare heart-and-lung disorder and is waiting for his last chance to get a transplant. See how Martin trusts God throughout his illness. Find out how he and Rebekka cope with the school bullies and how Rebekka finds out for herself who God is and what he is all about.

ISBN: 1-85792-425-8

TRAILBLAZERS

This is real life made as exciting as fiction! Anyone of these Trailblazer titles will take you into a world that you have never dreamed of. Have you ever wondered what it would be like to be a hero or heroine? What would it be like to really stand out for your convictions?

Meet these heroes and heroines and learn from their real life adventures:-

**George Muller
Hudson Taylor
Martyn Lloyd-Jones
Richard Wurmbrand
C.S. Lewis
Corrie Ten Boom
William Wilberforce**

Amazing people with amazing stories!

This is a series worth collecting.

TRAIL BLAZERS

The Children's Champion George Muller

by Irene Howat

If you were an orphan in the city of Bristol around 1850 then life was hard but if you got a place in one of George Muller's children's homes, the future was bright. It was like living in a big happy, loving family.

Yet when George Muller was young he was selfish and totally untrustworthy. Would you trust someone who stole from his own parents? So what changed him? Was it the spell in prison that stopped him stealing? Was it the tragic death of his mother that stopped the lies? Who changed the thief into a friend you could trust with millions of pounds?

Find out how God miraculously transformed one young man's life and how the orphaned children of Bristol find someone to love and to fight their corner. George is their champion.

ISBN: 1-85792-549-1

TRAIL BLAZERS

An Adventure Begins
Hudson Taylor

by Catherine Mackenzie

Hudson Taylor is well-known today as one of the first missionaries to go to China but he wasn't always a missionary. How did he become one then? What was his life like before China? In this book you will meet the Hudson Taylor who lived in Yorkshire as a young boy, fell desperately in love with his sister's music teacher and who struggled to gain independence as a teenager. You will also travel with Hudson to the Far East as he obeys God's call to preach the gospel to the Chinese people.

Witness the excitement as he and his sister visit London for the first time, sympathise with the heartache as Hudson leaves his family behind to go to China and experience the frustration as his sisters wait for his letters home.

Do you want to know more? Then read this book and let the adventure begin.

ISBN 1-85792-423-1

TRAIL BLAZERS

From Wales to Westminster
Martyn Lloyd-Jones

by his grandson
Christopher Catherwood

'Fire! Fire!' - A woman shouted frantically. However, as the villagers desperately organised fire fighting equipment the Lloyd-Jones family slept. They were blissfully ignorant that their family home and livelihood was just about to go up in smoke. Martyn, aged ten, was snug in his bed, but his life was in danger.

What happened to Martyn? Who rescued him? How did the fire affect him and his family? And why is somebody writing a book about Martyn in the first place? In this book Christopher Catherwood, Martyn's grandson, tells you about the amazing life of his grandfather, Dr. Martyn Lloyd-Jones. Find out about the young boy who trained to be a doctor at just sixteen years old. Meet the young man who was destined to become the Queen's surgeon and find out why he gave it all up to work for God. Read about Martyn Lloyd-Jones. He was enthusiastic and on fire for God. You will be, too, by the end of this book!

ISBN 1-85792-349-9

TRAIL BLAZERS

A Voice in the Dark
Richard Wurmbrand

by Catherine Mackenzie

'Where am I? What are you doing? Where are you taking me?' Richard's voice cracked under the strain. His heart was pounding so hard he could hardly breathe. Gasping for air he realized - this was the nightmare! Thoughts came so quickly he could hardly make sense of anything.

'I must keep control,' he said out loud. An evil chuckle broke out from beside him. 'You are no longer in control. We are your worst nightmare!'...

When Richard Wurmbrand is arrested, imprisoned and tortured, he finds himself in utter darkness. Yet the people who put him there discover that their prisoner has a light which can still be seen in the dark - the love of God. This incredible story of one man's faith, despite horrific persecution, is unforgettable and will be an inspiration to all who read it.

ISBN 1-85792-298-0

TRAIL BLAZERS

The Storyteller
C.S. Lewis

by Derick Bingham

C.S. Lewis loved to write stories even as a small child. He grew up to face grief when his mother died, fear when he fought in the First World War and finally love when he realised that God was a God of love and that his son Jesus Christ was the answer to his heartache.

C.S. Lewis brought this newly-discovered joy and wonder into his writings and became known world-wide for his amazing Narnia stories.

Read all about this fascinating man. Find out why his friends called him Jack and not his real name. Find out what C.S. Lewis was really like and discover how one of the greatest writers and academics of the twentieth century turned from atheism to God.

"A good introduction to my stepfather
C.S. Lewis"

Douglas Gresham

ISBN 1-85792-423-1

TRAIL BLAZERS

The Watchmaker's Daughter
Corrie ten Boom

by Jean Watson

If you like stories of adventure, courage and faith - then here's one you won't forget. Corrie loved to help others, especially handicapped children. But her happy lifestyle in Holland is shattered when she is sent to a Nazi concentration camp. She suffered hardship and punishment but experienced God's love and help in unbearable situations.

Her amazing story has been told worldwide and has inspired many people. Discover about one of the most outstanding Christian women of the 20th century.

ISBN 1-85792-116-X

TRAIL BLAZERS

The Freedom Fighter William Wilberforce

by Derick Bingham

'No! No!' cried the little boy, 'Please no! I want to stay with my mother!'
'Be quiet!' shouted the man who roughly pulled his mother from him. She was taken to a raised platform and offered for sale, immediately. The heartbroken mother was to be separated from her little boy for the rest of her life...

This was the fate of thousands of women and children in the days before slavery was abolished. One man fought to bring freedom and relief from the terrors of the slave trade; it took him forty-five years. His name was William Wilberforce. His exciting story shows the amazing effect his faith in Christ and his love for people had on transforming a nation.

'A story deserving to be told to a new generation.'
The Prime Minister the Rt. Hon. Tony Blair, M.P.

ISBN 1-85792-371-5

Look out for the next

TRAIL BLAZERS

title

ISOBEL KUHN

by
Irene Howat

CHRISTIAN FOCUS

Good books with the real message of hope!

Christian Focus Publications publishes biblically-accurate books for adults and children.

If you are looking for quality Bible teaching for children then we have a wide and excellent range of Bible story books - from board books to teenage fiction, we have it covered.

You can also try our new Bible teaching Syllabus for 3-9 year olds and teaching materials for pre-school children.

These children's books are bright, fun and full of biblical truth, an ideal way to help children discover Jesus Christ for themselves. Our aim is to help children find out about God and get them enthusiastic about reading the Bible, now and later in their life.

**Find us at our web page:
www.christianfocus.com**